Off the Dock

LAURIE HENDRY GRAYBAR

Answers are hidden inside family secrets.
She is driven to find the truth...
Even if it kills her.

ISBN: 1461172748
ISBN-13: 9781461172741

Library of Congress Control Number: 2011907696
CreateSpace, North Charleston, South Carolina

To my grandmothers, Louise and Mae Dell,
the strongest women I've ever known.

Preface

This book came to life for me as I was grasping the power of death from our earthly world. God's presence was most evident to me when I was faced with the mortality of my loved ones. Helplessly, my only choice was surrendering to the final stage of grief– which was acceptance. There was no negotiating; neither reasoning nor any amount of money could undo it...

It was done...

Case closed.

Acknowledgements

This project would have never come to fruition without the support of a network of people. It started as scribble in a journal, prescribed by a therapist during my grieving process. Once my husband Ben read it, he brought it to life with his never-ending encouragement.

Later, my daddy, Chuck Hendry, the greatest storyteller I know, nudged me along whenever my motor choked. There is no greater inspiration for a daughter than that of a father that believes she can do anything-even if she knows she can't.

My mama, Carol Hendry, always kept my coloring in the lines loving me unconditionally. She and my daddy are a great parent team, married forty-four years now.

Thanks to Sherry Harvey, my lifelong mentor, reminding me that creativity doesn't always need to be harnessed.

Laurie Lilliott, owner of *Taylor-Made Photography* and her beautiful, eldest daughter Hayden Lilliott (leg model) are responsible for my picturesque cover. Laurie demonstrated true Taylor County blue blood spirit.

As soon as she heard of my conflict for the professional cover needing to bring to life a rural beach dock, she grabbed Hayden and went straight to the Dekle Beach dock in Taylor County. It was there she used her photography gifts to create the perfect cover for OFF THE DOCK.

Linda Zimmerman helped transform my southern tone so that friends above the Mason-Dixon Line may understand the dialect.

As always, my childhood conspirators, Lisa Helm Ryan and Michael Morris (Author) cheered me to the finish-line, combining perfect measures of honesty and humor along the way. They maintained faith in me whenever I questioned myself.

Forever, I am thankful for Lexie Bethea, my assistant, friend, confidant and family without the same blood. You have never let me down.

Thank you Natalie Jimmine for allowing my dreams to seem possible again.

Finally, my beautiful sons, who are my promise of pixie dust for the future. Our boys indulged me in what came to be known as *Mama's quiet writing time on the porch. There is no word in the English language that is worthy of describing my love for my sons.*

Foreword

FROM AUTHOR MICHAEL MORRIS

For my entire life I have been entertained by the stories of Laurie Hendry Graybar. I've long wanted her to put pen to paper and she has finally done so with Off The Dock. It's a tour de force of small town secrets, unsolved murder and family loyalty – and as is typical with my childhood friend, she rewards the reader by tossing in some of her humor. And I'm so glad that she did.

Laurie and I share a hometown, family heritage and a love of storytelling. We come from a small North Florida town similar to the one Laurie presents in Off The Dock. We are not only close friends but we're even related through our Hendry lineage. Well, we are probably cousins four or five times removed, but where we come from, make no mistake about it – that still counts. Maybe our kinship helps to explain why we enjoy each other's humor so much. Whenever we are together we end up laughing – usually so loudly that everyone in the room turns to make sure that we haven't taken leave of our senses.

Even though Laurie tackles serious subjects in this novel, the humor that I love is evident in the characters – from Toot to Double Barrel – she captures the people of this magical world called Culley Cove. I've found that a good writer of dialogue, particularly dialect, is often a good mimic. Laurie is one of the best mimics I know — trust me, I've made myself sick laughing hysterically at her performances. I'm not surprised that she has populated this novel with some of the most interesting and eccentric characters I've read in some time.

Beyond humor, another similarity that Laurie and I share is our love of grandparents. Out of all of my friends, she is the one person I know who understands just how much grandparents can be a stable force of unconditional love and understanding. It is yet another bond that Laurie and I share. Therefore, it is no surprise that it's the grandmother in this novel, Gammy, who shines the brightest. Gammy comes to life with an energy that makes her jump off of the page. The very notion of a character who struggles to control her anger by quoting Bible verses — and who occasionally slips up with some cuss words, followed by even more scripture to make up for her loss of control — is worth the read!

Fix a glass of sweet tea, sit back and savor this tale that my friend has created – an enticing mixture of *Sweet Home Alabama and C.S.I.* Simply put, in my Cracker Florida way of talking, it's Pure D entertainment. And if you don't know what Pure D means then...well, you most certainly need to read this book.

Prologue

As we fell into family routines, he watched, mercilessly planning to shatter us to our core. He was incapable of empathy, yet fraught with intelligence. Charming and handsome it was effortless to conform himself into any situation with confidence. Over time, he developed a "predatory" lifestyle. His relationships were built for the sole purpose of manipulating or eliminating whomever got in his way.

That summer morning in 1978 plays in my mind with such vivid detail. It would be the last day of normalcy in my childhood. My memories have intertwined with Mama and Daddy's so that I can retell the story in its entirety.

My brother, Jackson, walked me to a birthday party. I was just ten years old when he kissed me good—bye. He never came home again. As I grew up, I was haunted by nightmares and hidden memories.

After years of therapy, I finally found a psychologist that wouldn't allow me to escape reality. This encouraged me to seek out answers hidden in family secrets.

It took me decades to face it. Little did I know that would only be the first step in finding the strength to unlock the past. Once I started exploring those dark places, I unwittingly awakened evil...

Now, it wants me.

Chapter 1

THE LAST MORNING
1978

I remember that morning as one of perfection. We never knew it would be the last day of normalcy before our lives shifted into chaos, guilt, and confusion.

The salty air played with the sand over the sleepy beach town of Culley Cove. Our family's quiet beach house was slowly awakening. The early sunlight steadied itself above the gulf.

High tide was coming into the channel. An occasional mullet would jump up and then plunge back into its salty home. It was a day like all of the ones before that. It was cheerful and somehow welcoming. At least, that was my perspective on our morning at that time.

Mama and Daddy's beach house was consumed with the smell of fatback bacon, homemade biscuits and coffee. Mama has always been one of the best cooks in North Florida, according to Pastor Caldwell's wife, Toot.

The kitchen windows were open and the sheer draperies moved back and forth as the beach air flirted with them. There was an ease about the house. Perhaps it was because it was the last sense of tranquility our family experienced before we felt that we were surviving rather than actually living.

Mama stood in her terrycloth robe over the stove. She was watching the grease brown the fat as Daddy popped her soft bottom with his newspaper.

She gave him a look of flirtatious disapproval and then pointed her large eyes to the kitchen table. This was her nonverbal clue for him to sit and behave...which was behavior trained by repetition from eighteen years of marriage.

My mama always carried a certain elegance that made her different from the other Culley Cove women. She made a point of having her hair in place even for morning breakfast. She was petite in stature but had a presence about her that made her seem important. She was a strong woman with a great deal of pride. Mostly, she was proud to have married into the Churchill family and to have my brother and me as her children. She felt that this was her greatest honor. The only excuse for our wrongdoing was generally that someone else was jealous of us. She had managed to convince herself of this delusion when we were both there with her and Daddy. Mama was good at making herself believe what she needed to in order to survive.

Mama could make a bathrobe seem somehow proper when she wore it. She would keep the sash tied just right, and her slippers would always match the underlying pajamas. She would faintly brush powder on her face before so much as going to the bathroom in the morning. Mama said it just wasn't right for any woman past the age of twenty—five to leave her house without powder on her face and a good girdle on her behind.

Trust me, she still reminds me of my failure to do this on a regular basis. She thinks that I am in a secret conspiracy against her to become a hippie. You see, I love nature, which takes me outdoors most of the time. Mama wanted me to sit at the piano stool and stay in hair bows for most of my childhood. It just didn't seem to fit me.

Daddy was always eager to announce that he had landed the prettiest woman on Culley Cove. Whenever he said this, Mama would bashfully look at him and blush. She knew, as did my brother and I, that Daddy had been quite the catch himself.

He was a star football player for our North Florida team in high school. Daddy could have gone to college and played for Clemson but instead he decided to stay in Culley and marry Mama.

Many a woman had thought he was one of the most handsome boys Culley Cove produced. Daddy had taken his place at the Churchill Marina after marrying my mama. He had done well for our family, adding more to the place than Pee—Paw had started.

My mama and daddy, Sugar and Titus Churchill, grew up in Culley Cove as their families had for two generations back. Everybody called my mama Shug. This was short for Sugar, which is what Daddy nicknamed her after their first kiss in grade school. It had stuck through the years.

They knew every single person on the island well enough to drop by any time, sip sweet tea, and tell a story or two. We never even considered locking our doors back then. The fact of the matter was, if somebody needed something badly enough, we would have wanted them to come in and get it. They would tell us later and replace it. We were that trusting and innocent.

Pastor Smitty Caldwell and his wife, Toot, were the best fellowshipping leaders of the Culley Baptist Church you could find. They kept us all so well connected with one another.

I tell you, if a Culley Cove neighbor should experience hardship, Toot Caldwell would convene a church group in short order.

They would be at your door within hours of your bad news with the county's best pies, collard greens, and fried chicken. After eating yourself into a natural coma, the visitors would start flocking to your back door. We were taught to share our own problems and that would help neighbors not feel so alone.

Until this particular morning, we knew just as we knew the sun would rise and set that we would have friends, food, and family at the end of each day. If you've never had that kind of security, you won't believe it. Trust me; it did exist. I remember it and still treasure what we had in those days.

In the seventies, there was no cable way out in Culley Cove. Each night, everyone watched the local Channel 6 news station right after supper.

Mrs. Mira Hicks was front and center of the television screen every evening at 6:00. Her hair was perfectly teased as she twanged away the highlights of church fundraising events, local tides and the charter boat catches. The only crime she ever broadcast was an occasional prank played out in neighboring beach communities by the young'ins.

I can still hear Gammy as she would watch old Mira in the evenings.

"Bless her heart, I know she don't know better, but Mira's hair is gettin' taller and taller. Pretty soon, it ain't gone fit on the TV screen no more if she don't watch it," Gammy would say with a graveled giggle.

Our family had a particular interest in the fishing news because Pee—Paw owned one of the largest boat marinas on the Gulf Coast of Florida. My daddy and his siblings all owned a piece of that huge marina. They chartered trips, sold fish, repaired boats, and stored them for seasonal sportsmen.

They had even opened up a special place to schedule hunting lodge retreats for the local men on family-owned property outside Taylor County. Pee—Paw had done well for our family, but we never spoke of it. There was no money—flaunting from us. That wouldn't be proper.

Like their neighbors, Mama and Daddy lived by the good book and dedicated their lives to hard work and raising their offspring. Mama taught Sunday school and helped Daddy with his part at the Churchill Marina. My brother Jackson and I were as proud as our parents and grandparents that our family was a deep—rooted part of Culley Cove.

Our Churchill family was part of a group known as the *Original* 8 or *T08*. These were the first eight families who claimed rights to the beachfront property for pennies on the dollar in 1916. Way back, this specific beach property was not considered marketable commercial real estate on account of my Great—Uncle Fiddler.

Bless his heart, he had what, at the time, seemed to be a novel idea. He ran sewage disposal pipes from his outhouse through the canal to his crop and then back to the waterway.

He liked it so well he started hooking up all of the Culley residents to it. They were creating their very own fertilizer for their crops. The vegetables were flourishing and you couldn't beat the price either. You might say Great—Uncle Fiddler became famous in our backwoods beach town.

The way Gammy and Pee—Paw tell it, he was a master thinker, like all of the Churchill men. He had come up with this clever dual sewage fertilization system, planning to make him a national success.

Well, he kind of did, but not in the way he had hoped. Years later, when the land developers were considering Culley Cove for a new seaport, they were appalled. They felt that human waste feeding directly into the canal was disgusting, not industrious. There was quite a bit of negative press. Several big agencies went out to Culley to investigate. Pee—Paw said poor Uncle Fiddler had a heart attack and died right there beside his outhouse. He was right in the middle of explaining his creation to the water cleanup groups.

Culley Cove, now pristine and private, had once been one fine mess to clean up. Our ancestors had been teased about living on *Culley Cove: Where the Finest Fecal Matter Is Made and Reused.*

Gammy once heard some man saying that at the city feed store. She walked right up to him and hit him in the back of the head with her handbag. "I showed him," Gammy said as she told us about it later that day.

* * *

Mama and Daddy were excited that morning because my brother, Jackson, had come home early from his Baptist Revival Camp. He had gone every year since he was twelve.

Now, at the age of sixteen, he told Mama he was just plain bored. This in itself didn't surprise them because Jackson had always been a bit high-strung. The school used to have to call Mama regularly when he was younger. Later, they fancied up the title of it to attention deficit hyperactivity disorder or ADHD. My gammy huffed over that title because it had the word "disorder" in it. "Foot," she would say, "hyperactivity is a gift, if you ask me. I have been hyper my whole life. It's the hyper ones that have the greatest ideas, ya know?"

She would wink at me every time she made this statement, because she was as certain as the rest of our family that I was a carrier of this bouncy gene. Gammy was our crusader. She said what she thought and could not care less how others might perceive it.

My brother was outgoing and the greatest storyteller of our generation. Daddy says Jackson came home early because he got wind of Uncle Taft coming back from college that weekend to visit.

You see, Uncle Taft is Daddy's baby brother or Gammy and Pee-Paw's accident, depending on who is tellin' the story. He and Jackson were as thick as thieves. Taft was older than Jackson and had always taken him under his wing. Jackson in turn protected Taft from some of the criticisms that he experienced growing up in Culley. Taft, the youngest Churchill among daddy's siblings, was not as masculine as most of the boys in Culley were expected to be. He could do physical labor as well as any of them, but his interests were different. He preferred the piano as opposed to playing football. It was one of those observations we made, but no one in the family spoke of it. Jackson and Uncle Taft always had a reciprocating relationship. Jackson would protect Uncle Taft from the bullies at school while Uncle Taft tutored Jackson with his academics.

Daddy says even today that Taft coming home, combined with my crying on the phone each time Jackson called sealed the deal for his surprise homecoming. Daddy doesn't realize how much those words pierce me, because I wish I hadn't encouraged Jackson to come home early.

I was peacefully sleeping upstairs in my cupcake— like bedroom. Mama Shug and Gammy Churchill had customized pink and white bedding and drapes for me.

Pee—Paw and Uncle Skeeter had made my wooden headboard in the shape of a firefly. I remember that I had left my butterfly lamp on every night since Jackson had been away. I missed him so much that summer. I was counting the days until his return and was so happy that he came home earlier than expected.

The breakfast smells had me starting to stir in my sleep. Elvis, my little rescue mutt, had begun licking my face with his puppy breath in hopes of snatching some bacon for himself. I could hear Mama and Daddy talking quietly downstairs as the bacon tickled my nose.

Jackson tiptoed to the outside of my door, waiting for just the perfect second to surprise me.

Mama Shug followed Jackson upstairs. She was two steps behind him training him with exaggerated warnings.

"Now, Jackson," she whispered, "don't be too aggressive with her! I swear you'll scare her to death! I mean it," Mama warned.

Suddenly, in perfect teenage persona, he burst in and jumped over onto my bed, tickling me.

I popped my eyelids open and squealed, "*Jaack-soooon*, you're here, you're really here!"

I laughed until I was out of breath from his tickling combined with the excitement of him being back home.

"Yes, ma'am," he said, grinning from ear to ear. I wanted to pinch myself to make sure I wasn't still dreaming. Our house had been way too quiet with my brother away. He had such a special way of making everything come to life.

"I couldn't stay away from my best girl that long," Jackson said, throwing me back for more tickling.

Elvis barked and hopped over us excitedly.

"Hey, scruffy mutt," Jackson said, talking to the silly dog.

He had found the poor neglected stray for me weeks before he left for camp. I love dogs just about as much as I do people, and so did my brother.

"You know you are my favorite sister, Caroline," he said as he messed up my hair.

"I am your *only* sister!" I corrected with a pout.

It was then I noticed that he had used the camp as an excuse to get away from Mama long enough to grow his hair out.

"Your hair is almost as long as Mama's," I said, exaggerating reality as I touched his long strands.

He put his finger to his lips, hoping to quiet me before Mama chimed in on the subject.

"OK," he said, "I had just had enough of the Baptist Fellowship for this summer," he confided. "I decided to come home a little early and give my favorite girl a surprise."

Mama interjected from the doorway, "You need to go by the barbershop today and get that hippie hair cut off."

Then she tilted her head toward Jackson to exaggerate her point.

"Mama, I thought you could braid it for me later today," he said while winking at my daddy.

Mama looked at him and said, "Jackson Churchill, you will be the death of me."

There was one truth about Jackson that no one had to second-guess, and that was his adoration of me. He had always understood me. It was one of my greatest gifts in life to have him for my brother, if only for a short while.

We had been close since I was born ten years before. Even with the age gap, our spirits were connected. He loved shocking Mama more than anything. I was the perfect accomplice for that.

Jackson had just turned sixteen yet carried a maturity about him far beyond his years. Gammy had called him an *old soul*. He was just that. Jackson could always see the glass half full and tried to help everybody around him do the same. He was a natural at making everyone feel special. That was one of Jackson's gifts in this world, and I loved him for it.

The strange thing is that it wasn't until his last day with us that he ever seemed skeptical of anybody. It's something that we have thought about for many years. Somehow, Jackson must have felt in his bones that day that something sadistic was around him. He seemed to have had his thinking changed somewhat at camp that summer.

Our Jackson could light up a room from the time he walked in. His good looks and congeniality instantly made him likeable to most people. Jackson had sandy hair that was always sun-kissed from being on the boats. His skin was flawless and perfectly tanned. More than all of these attributes, it was Jackson's smile that could move everyone. It was the warmest, most sincere beauty that said more than any word. The morning of his return, he lit our old house up like a Christmas tree. His laughter and silliness was so comforting to us all.

He had his hyper times like me. Perhaps this is why he understood me so well. He knew that boys could somehow pull it off. Girls were generally considered awkward or accident—prone if they were hyperactive. That was the case with me and always had been.

Jackson loved telling me to be true to myself. It was something the guidance counselor at his school had once told him and he liked it. At least, that is where he said he had heard it. He said that a lot that last summer.

In those days, Mama Shug dressed me up like a pastry. It was a rare day to find me without a huge bow perched in my blond locks. Sometimes my dresses had flowers on them half as big as Daddy's boat motor. When I would come down those stairs dressed up in those frilly clothes, Jackson would laugh so hard he would fall on the floor. He used to stop laughing, stand back up, and then fall to the floor laughing again.

"Mama, don't do that to sister!" he would say to Mama as she ignored him entirely.

He loved nothing more than taking me out to the muddy creek behind Gammy and Pee—Paw's when the tide was out. He would encourage me to get filthy from head to toe. Gammy used to call Mama just before we started walking home to warn her. I can still see her head cocked to support the telephone.

"Sugar, ya better start your yard hose," Gammy used to say, "The young'ins are comin' that way. They are filthy as pigs too."

Mama wouldn't let us in the house before she stood in the yard and shot us down with the hose. We would squeal as the ice—cold water sprayed the mud off our bodies. She would clean us, and Jackson would hit the ground, getting dirty all over again.

Under her breath, Mama would pray that she could find patience not to beat us to death. He would point over at her and giggle with me. It never took long for Mama to finally join the laughing, which made it even funnier.

No matter how excited I would get, Jackson seemed to embrace it. Lord, I miss those days. I miss my brother, Jackson.

Chapter 2

THE SECRET BOX
1978

M ama and Daddy were watching us from the doorway of my room that morning. It felt safe and normal. We were laughing and teasing each other. Even Elvis seemed to be happy about Jackson's early return. That fool dog was dancing around the bed, wagging his crooked tail and yelping. Whenever he would yelp, Jackson would chime in, mimicking him.

Finally, Mama Shug interjected, "Ya'll better come on 'less you want cold breakfast this morning."

Jackson made a shush gesture to Mama, who bugged her eyes at him as if to say, "*I never.*"

That's when Jackson got our attention by covering his lips with his finger. Then, he ever so slowly reached underneath my bed. He pulled out a wrapped box as if it were a magic trick. Daddy bumped Mama, silently giggling at the cuteness of the situation. I grabbed it and sat up on my knees, crinkling the white linen nightgown. I popped off the bow and ripped through the wrapping paper.

"Caroline, Lord, slow down, child," Mama said, looking on. Mama knew how I had trouble controlling my energy.

Inside was the most beautiful wooden box with a firefly design on the top. I pulled it out and just stared at it. It was so pretty, and Jackson had made it for me, which made it even more perfect in my eyes.

"Jackson!" I screamed. "It's beautiful!"

I wrapped my arms tightly around his neck, not wanting to let go.

"I made it myself," he explained eagerly. "I cut the wood and hinged the top on it real tight so it won't break. I molded the edges to make it pretty for my princess."

He was carefully watching my response to the gift. I could see the pride in his eyes as I examined it with my mouth wide open.

"Then I used an engraving bit on a rotary tool," he continued, "to put the firefly on top. 'Cause I know how much you love them."

He had even painted it pink and routed the words CAROLINE CHURCHILL on the side for me. It was clear that he had taken his time to make this a special present, and I was so proud of it.

"This isn't just a box to keep prissy stuff in," he said as Mama winced at this comment from the doorway.

Jackson explained, "You keep special things in it. Write down your thoughts, and then later go back and read 'em. It's amazin' how different whatever you write about will change by the next time you read it."

"It sure helps me think things over better," he said while smiling.

He looked up at Daddy for approval.

Daddy was beaming with pride. The feeling that your children love each other, and they are good inside has a way of making a parent proud.

"You know, Caroline, Jackson explained, "this is a Churchill tradition of sorts. Uncle Taft taught me about these boxes. He's outgrown his now that he is a big—shot college boy."

"Little sister, you know what?" he said. "This helps bouncy people like us realize if we held our tongue, we wouldn't say some of what we do in the first place," he whispered, gesturing toward Mama.

"Jackson Churchill," Mama piped in, "I think before I speak. You just don't always like what I say!"

"Ahhh, and my point is made," he said while laughing in sync with Daddy.

Mama huffed to herself in fun.

Refocusing us on the box again, he said, "What you wanna do is dig a hole and bury it after you put your secret treasures inside. Then, every time you want to add something to it or look at what's already there, you dig it back up again."

Then, he raised his pointer finger to me and said, "Change your location so no one ever finds it. It's your secret safety deposit box by the sea."

He made it seem so magical and mysterious to me. Then again, my brother made everything seem special. That was his gift.

The expression on his face was cheerful that morning. I found that he had taught me something about himself and our family. He, once again, made me feel as if I was a part of something larger than life.

Then, he added something that at the time seemed unimportant. "I made one for myself last summer," he said. "I put a shark on the top of mine."

I looked at him secretively and whispered, "Did you bury yours, Jackson?"

"Of course I did," he replied. "I keep all of my secrets in it too, but you will never find it. You have to keep changing your location."

"Jackson, I swear, don't have her diggin' out in the dirt all the time," Mama yelled from the hallway, shaking her head.

Then, we were sheep—dogged downstairs by Mama Sugar reminding us that she had cooked us a breakfast fit for royalty.

The once quiet house had come to life while Jackson entertained us with one hilarious camping story after another.

He had such high energy...and could narrate a story so you felt like you were sitting right there in the middle

18

of it. I swear, he was the type of talker who could make you smell and taste his stories.

Mama Shug found herself constantly reminding him to quiet down. She did this by daintily holding her pointer finger up to her mouth and giving him that bug—eyed look.

She followed this with the gesture of holding up his mug of coffee. You see, Gammy once heard from some ladies at the bookstore that high—strung kids should drink coffee. Yes, it would actually calm them down. By the time Gammy's Oldsmobile hit the driveway in Culley, she reported the news to Mama Shug. Jackson had quickly become a coffee connoisseur of sorts ever since.

They had never put Jackson on medication, because in the seventies no one believed you should. All those hippies were taking drugs, after all. *Why in heaven's name would we give it to our young'ins was Gammy's rationalization on the subject.* It sure sounded sensible to Mama and the Culley Baptist choir ladies, so they agreed.

I remember that Jackson's stories were getting me wound up that morning. I was slipping Elvis bacon scraps underneath the table while Jackson performed one animated story after another.

Mama Shug was wiping tears from her eyes from laughing so hard listening to him. Daddy leaned back in his chair, rubbing his full belly. He was beaming with pride because he knew Jackson got his storytelling ability from him.

"Uncle Taft is due in this afternoon," Daddy said slowly in his deep voice. "Gammy is on fire about everybody showing up to give him a proper welcome."

Mama asked, "How did Uncle Taft do as summer camp counselor for the week he filled in for the director?"

"He was great," Jackson answered eagerly.

"In fact," he said, smacking food in his mouth, "most of the campers thought he should replace Landon Caldwell."

Mama scowled.

"Now, don't ya'll dare go and insult the pastor's son," Mama said. "That Landon is about to start theology school."

She paused for the drama.

"If ya'll don't know, that means studyin' the Bible," she said, clearing her throat to sound dignified.

Then mama held her cup in front of her mouth and asked the big question, "So, has our Taft found a nice college girl yet?"

Jackson rolled his eyes, because mama was all too aware that Taft had only dated girls for the two proms he had attended.

"My baby brother is a unique soul," daddy said in defense of his brother. "I think that's why he studied so much in school and never took a likin' to ball. He will probably preach the gospel one day."

"Titus, it's priests that don't marry women, not pastors," mama said looking seriously at daddy.

Jackson changed the subject.

"I can't wait to see Uncle Taft tonight," he said while smacking on a mouthful of eggs.

"We had kind of a blowup at camp a few weeks ago," he explained. "I really owe him an..." he stopped mid-sentence and looked away.

It seemed he thought better of detailing this any further with Mama and Daddy.

He went right on to say, "*Oooh*, do I have a story for him tonight," as he laughed thinking of it.

"So, Mama, is Taft looking after the Baileys' house this weekend?" he asked, "or am I supposed to do it?"

"Jackson!" Mama said glancing up at him, "I'm so glad you reminded me.

"You are to do it," Mama continued. "Double Barrel and Thyra Bailey have been worried half to death about their dogs while they are travelin'. Since you have been at camp and Taft is in college now, they struggle to find good kids to look after those dogs of theirs," Mama said. "Double Barrel solicited some unnamed kids from the church to help 'em. He and Thyra say that them young'ins weren't feedin' the poor dogs enough. Those old birddogs started to look like bags of bones.

"Thyra says poor Double Barrel was out of nerve pills last week when it happened and had turned to the liquor bottle."

Mama was just shaking her head and sipping out of her cup.

"Men just get so carried away with their stresses," she said. "That old devil in hell just beats on their backs."

Daddy looked up and winked at Jackson.

The Baileys had four sons who all played college football. They had two at FSU, one at Clemson, and one at Alabama. Double Barrel and his wife, Thyra Bailey, drove their tattered Winnebago all over to watch the games each week. It was during these times that Taft or Jackson would look after their dogs and house. Thyra liked them to turn different lights on inside the house to make it seem as if someone was home.

Since the Baileys' boys played ball for big—name college teams, it had become a fad for some of the kids in the neighboring beach communities to drive over and toilet paper their oak trees. It was harmless, but drove poor ole' Double Barrel Bailey nuts.

When the Winnebago was gone, the pranksters knew it was safe to unroll the Charmin on the branches.

The Bailey property sat right beside my great—grandparents' vacant house. God rest their souls. Uncle Taft was to inherit that from Gammy and Pee—Paw after college graduation.

"I'm going to Nita's birthday party tonight!" I yelled, seeking attention.

I had gotten up and started inappropriately dancing around the kitchen table, feeling the escalating excitement within me.

"You are?" Jackson asked, as if he hadn't known.

"Uhhh huuuuh," I said, still running around the table.

"*Caroline, I swear, if you don't sit down at this table like a lady!*" Mama said while glaring at me.

"She's excited, Mama," Daddy defended me playfully. "Aren't you, baby girl?"

"Uh huh," I peeped. "We are staying up all night long tonight. We might even sneak out," I continued, feeling as if I had passed gas in church with the realization of giving my mama too much information.

"What did you say?" Mama lurched forward in her chair, putting her mug down.

"All right, all right," Daddy said, grabbing me gently to settle down in his lap.

"Young lady, don't you ever misbehave if you can help it," he said. "Especially under somebody else's roof when they think enough of you and us to have you in their home. Do you understand me?" Daddy asked as he lightly touched my cheek.

"Yees, sir," I answered in a low apologetic voice.

I was batting my blue eyes to the best of my ability. Daddy could do nothing more than plant a kiss on my cheek while looking sheepishly at Mama.

"I swear, Titus Churchill, that girl has you wrapped all the way around her finger," Mama snapped. "She's about as 'hyperactive' as Jackson." She said this in a loud whisper as if we couldn't hear it.

"Ya'll girls better behave," Mama reminded, stretching her eyelids open to punctuate her warning.

"The last thing I need is for Suzie Ledbetter to run around the Baptist Church telling everybody about my high—strung kids again," she said.

"All right, Mama," Daddy hushed her.

He never wanted to hear anything about us except how perfect we were. He thought our high spirits separated us from the other bland children we brought to his house.

"Don't you go and hush me up, Titus Churchill! You know that Suzie Ledbetter enjoys finding any way possible to talk about our hyper kids. Lord, forgive me for saying it, but her Nita is not much of a looker."

Mama then made a dramatic pause.

"Her Ustus is slow as honey runnin' out the bottle on Sunday. Lord love 'em all and I do, Titus, but we can't have our children giving her reason to criticize."

She rose from the table, tightening her bathrobe sash and collecting dishes.

As she walked to the sink, she whispered, "Bless them all, God willing, and forgive me. We are just so blessed, so blessed, yes we are."

I remember that, because I believe that would be the last time Mama would say that in her life.

Chapter 3

CAREFUL WHAT YOU SAY
1978

Daddy was shaking his head in a teasing fashion, crossing his eyes at us children so that Mama couldn't see him.

"I can see you, Titus. I have eyes in the back of my head," she said slowly, never turning away from scrubbing the dishes in the sink.

We were giggling at her as Daddy stepped out of his chair and went to the sink to hug her from behind.

"Honey, I married you because of your two extra back-head eyes. Of course, it didn't hurt that you could give me these two hard-headed, high-strung children. Don't you know that by now?" Daddy said, laughing.

Jackson and I were snickering at them while continuing to watch as Mama finally joined in. Daddy gave her several loud peck kisses before directing everyone to start helping clear the table.

"So, princess," Jackson said, "do you have any secrets to put in your firefly box this morning?"

"Yeah!" I squealed. "I have to go and get my secrets together."

"*Nobody* come to my room, OK?"

I still remember the sound of my bare feet slapping the wooden stairs and the loud slam of my bedroom door. I could picture Mama's expression and Jackson's joy at my noisy actions.

Mama tells the story about their conversation after my retreat upstairs. She, Daddy, and Jackson had stayed in the kitchen to clean the dishes.

"It was real nice of you to make that box for your sister, son," Daddy said as Mama handed him another dish to dry.

"It sure was, Jackson," Mama agreed and followed up explaining her morning comments.

"Now, I don't want you or Caroline to ever think I don't love your fire and spirit," Mama explained. "Ya'll got it from Gammy no doubt and Lord knows how much I love her. It's my job as your mama to try and help you harness it by warning you. Do you understand?" She stopped working at the sink and looked Jackson right in the eyes.

Daddy was smiling at them, knowing that Mama always said what she thought and later felt guilty and tried to smooth it over. He also knew that his son had this awareness and would likely have some fun playing with her guilt.

"Mama, I came to terms with my hyperactivity in the third grade," Jackson said. "Remember when Mrs. Hardy made me stand in the corner of the room with a bar of soap in my mouth for fifteen straight minutes?"

"Jackson, how could I ever forget it?"

"All for telling stories the same way I had done right here in this kitchen ever since I could remember," Jackson continued.

"Not during a math lesson, Jackson!"

"Boy, when she told me she was calling you about it, I thought I would die right there," Jackson said, thinking about it. "You remember that, Mama?" he asked.

"Oh, yes, yes," Mama said in her breathy voice.

"God bless her soul. She was so jealous of you because her children, bless them," Mama searched for words, "were just, well, simple!" Mama finished, shaking her head as if she had forced herself to say it.

"Now, Mama, you have to give the woman some credit," Jackson reminded. "After all, I was the child that put that huge rat snake in the teachers' lounge toilet."

He continued, "Mrs. Hardy was the unfortunate teacher to lift the lid. We could hear that poor old thang screamin' all the way down in the gymnasium. I'm pretty sure she didn't like me too much after that."

"Jackson, the old lady fainted right there with her drawers down," Mama said, thinking back on it. "The other teachers, some of whom were men, saw her privates!" she scowled, thinking of the horrific details.

Daddy and Jackson gave each other high fives as they roared with laughter.

"You are more than half the problem yourself, Titus Churchill!" she reprimanded.

"It took half of the Churchill family to get you out of that one, or you would be perched up at some military school today, Jackson!" Her voice was now getting high pitched with excitement.

"So, Caroline is going to the Ledbetters' tonight to sleep over?" Jackson diverted the conversation while sipping his coffee.

"Yes, it's Nita's tenth birthday, and Mr. Ledbetter is finally allowing the poor child to have a real party," Mama said sadly.

"Is he OK?" Jackson asked.

Daddy started. "Ole Ledbetter is just from a big city up north. He doesn't appreciate the gift of gab, but that don't make him a bad person, son."

Mama was shaking her head in agreement.

"Jackson, remember your Bible," Mama said. "John 6:37, 'All that the Father gives me will come to me and whoever comes to me I will never cast out.'"

"Mama, I ain't in church!" Jackson said.

"I am *not* in church," she corrected as Daddy smiled at Jackson.

Then, Jackson told them something kind of strange. Not strange at the time, but much later it seemed just that.

"There are lots of weird things going on in this old world. We've got to remember that we're not always just going to be protected in our little Culley," Jackson said thoughtfully.

"That's why we live where we do, darlin'. We know that here in Culley, we can protect ya'll," Mama said.

"Mama, I know Caroline and Nita Ledbetter are best friends. Nita is as sweet as can be. Her brother Ustus is kind of a weirdo, though. Mr. Ledbetter seems strange too. Lately, I've heard about a lot of stuff going on in the world that scares me. We need to be careful, Mama. I don't think Caroline should be over there much when he is around," Jackson said seriously.

"What in the world kind of turn-your-nose-up-at-the-Bible kind of young'in am I raising here, Jackson Churchill?" Mama yelped. Daddy giggled, darting his eyes back and forth to each of them as he grabbed the last piece of bacon off a dirty plate.

"I know you know what I mean, Mama." Jackson had not joked or backed down as he usually did with her.

"Some people ain't right, Mama. It's my duty to tell you that as your son," he said very slowly.

At this, Mama Shug looked at Jackson disapprovingly.

"Nita Ledbetter and your sister are best friends. We can't help that her daddy doesn't socialize or worship. Maybe it's our job to have influence on the poor man."

Mama reached over and touched his long strands of hair, shaking her head in disapproval. She reminded him of his Christian obligation that she had forgotten herself just minutes before.

She said, in a whispered voice as if they were perched on a church pew rather than in their own house, "Poor Ustus has always been off-center, but he is a sweet boy who comes from another good Baptist family." Her voice now escalated to a full-power whisper.

Jackson's response to Mama had been simply, "Ten-four, Mama."

My mama would spend the rest of her life remembering this conversation and feeling guilt for the way she had handled it.

Chapter 4

DREAMS TO REALITY
1998

My husband shook me to consciousness from the recurring nightmare that welcomed itself into my sleep world. I had been mumbling something about a secret safety deposit box by the sea and a man at the Baileys' house.

My eyes opened to the reflecting moonlight on his face. As I acknowledged consciousness, I noticed he was offering me a glass of water.

"Thank you," I said as I slurped down the water.

The glowing green numbers of the digital clock read 3:40 a.m. My husband, Cleeve, said nothing. My nightmares were a part of our lives. I had experienced them on and off since we met in college. My mind continued to bring my brother, Jackson, back to life again and again, with clues about what may have happened to him. There were things that I couldn't remember while I was awake, but in sleep I had vivid recollections.

My most recent therapist told Cleeve that my mind wanted to save Jackson. The shrink was convinced that for this reason alone my subconscious created dreams that started with the same morning we all remembered, but ended with more detail than anyone else had recounted. The guilt that I carried on my shoulders for going to Nita's tenth birthday party had overwhelmed me.

Jackson had come home early because I cried for him when he called from camp. I am the one who told him about Uncle Taft's visit, hoping that he would surprise us and come back early.

If only he had stayed there at the Baptist Revival Camp in 1978, he would have never come back to Culley that day and walked me to Nita's party.

I always blamed myself, and I knew that it must have crossed everyone's mind over the years. In the Churchill family, however, no one would ever speak it. They had doted on me as if I had become a piece of fine china. It was as if they believed that whatever had happened to Jackson might also happen to me.

* * *

At Jackson's service, Pastor Smitty Caldwell stood at the pulpit in his brown leisure suit. He was a stout man with a jolly sort of look about him. He seemed unable to find his sense of peace. Even he, our pastor, was visibly shaken that day. I would never forget his words as I looked on with one eye hidden behind Pee-Paw's arm.

"Jackson Churchill loved his sister, Caroline, with all of his heart.

"Why, his last journey on this earthly ground was carryin' her over to her friend Nita's birthday party. Brother and sister walkin' through the trails right here on our beautiful beach. He would have certainly wanted his life to end instead of hers on that day."

I still remember Mama Sugar just burrowing her head down into Daddy's chest. Her cry was so primal that the entire church seemed to rock with her.

They all trembled with the realization that this could have been any of them. I felt eyes burning on me as if Jackson was protecting me when he was taken.

I knew that all he had done was walk me to Nita's. I also knew that he would have traded himself for me. He loved me that much. I didn't know then and still don't know today if anyone, including Jackson, understood that I would have given myself up for him just the same.

* * *

My husband was slowly rubbing my back in the bleak silence of our bedroom.

"It's happening again, Cleeve," I whispered as if to hide the words from the air.

"I know, I know," he said softly.

Cleeve wasn't big on words or expression. I think this was because he was from the North. Whatever had drawn me to a man who didn't completely understand my passion for drama would always confuse me somewhat. What I had in drama he had in patience.

I knew that God had a plan when He had us meet in college. Nita had taken me out for my birthday on campus the night I met my husband.

He walked by me at a keg party and accidently bumped into me. Then Cleeve had quietly apologized for the mishap. At that, I retaliated by pushing him as hard as I could, until he fell to the floor. He had stared at me as if questioning my sanity.

I reached out to help him up, knowing that I had acted on impulse. It was then I noticed his perfect green eyes. He went home with me that night and we had been together every night since. He knew I was a fireball and often spoke before thinking. Cleeve had always been entertained by my quick thoughts and sense of humor.

We're opposites, but somehow it always made the wheel turn. He understood the pain in my heart about Jackson, how it likely changed me from who I would have become. He also knew that I love those that I love with a vengeance. Our son has been the center of my world since birth. Cleeve has enjoyed my drama where our child is concerned.

He had gone to therapy with me. Also, my family warned him almost weekly to take good care of me 'cause, as Gammy Churchill put it, "She is fragile since she lost Jackson." I knew that Cleeve was a rational person, and was certain that in his mind he concluded from Gammy's words, "It's been twenty years. Can we move on, people?"

It was now time for my ritual wee morning walk out to my old wooden dock. This had become my sanctuary to sort my busy thoughts and guilt. I tried to remember things that I was certain I had forgotten. There was a lock on my brain that would protect me from thoughts that may crush me.

I arose from my bed, followed by Tripod, my three-legged rescue dog. He hobbled along beside me as if he were a caretaker at a funeral announcing..."It's time."

"You're never gonna learn to sleep if you always give in to the nightmares," Cleeve said softly. "Don't go to the dock staying up all night," he continued.

He said this as he pulled the quilts back over his body while watching me. The old ceiling fan made its slow whooping sound as we looked at each other.

Cleeve knew that he spoke out of an obligation to do the right thing. He had no doubt, the second my body stood, no matter what he said, I was going to my dock and would likely watch the sun rise there.

He also knew that one of my most daring accomplishments had become a morning routine for me. You see,

I jumped off my dock into the smooth morning water. I did this just before the sun cast too much light on me.

I wouldn't want our neighbors, Double Barrel and Thyra Bailey, to catch me in my underwear. They had trees and brush that blocked their view of my dock back then, but still, I never would jump in full light.

I stripped right down to my drawers and bra and jumped into the water. It wasn't a pretty sight I'm sure. Don't misunderstand me; I am not an ugly woman. In fact, I can still stop a grocery bagger or two at the Winn-Dixie. My blond hair and blue eyes have maintained their charm. Mama gave me her good genes of clear skin, for which I am grateful. I have to watch my indulgence of the Little Debbies, as so many of us do, when that old metabolism starts finding yellow yield signs.

Since I gave birth to Wit, however, I am not what they call hot in my bathing suit. I think it's more of the comparison in my mind of what the body was and how gravity has become its sidekick. I wouldn't even want Cleeve to see me in wet undergarments with my hair plastered to my head and no makeup on after these swims.

My jumps are my way of proving to myself that I am still strong inside. The dock isn't just some skimpy little plank. No, Pee-Paw meant business when he had this structure built. It's long enough that when I am out on it, I appear like a speck of dust. Jumping gives me the ability to demonstrate my loud clumsiness that only Jackson had appreciated in me.

Whenever I jump off my dock like this, I swear I can hear him laughing with me in my head. He would enjoy thinking of what Mama would say about me swimming in the early morning with just underclothes on. It feels so good to connect with him on this level of fantasy.

Going off the dock is my way of telling the world that had broken me, "I fear nothing. I win."

If only for the minute of the jump and the brief swim back to shore, I am brave. Me, Caroline Churchill Burton can face her truths fearlessly. That is true for those moments even though I don't know all of my truths.

Crazy old Tripod jumps right along with me each morning. He grunts and struggles with those three legs, but seems to enjoy our little exercise. I always tell Cleeve that is what this is: exercise. I know it's about breaking free and taking one of the few risks I can find.

Once Cleeve slipped up and told Gammy about my morning plunges in my panties. She had laughed and shown such pride in my bravery.

You have to understand that my gammy is the most courageous woman on this earth. She is full of life and energy. She cares only about what makes sense to her. I love her for that.

"That's my girl!" Gammy said proudly about my morning panty crusades.

"Fearless," she said, smiling at me. There are few relationships in this old world like that of a grandparent to a grandchild. If you are lucky enough to experience that as I was, you will likely never forget it.

"You're just like your gammy," she would say, laughing.

It was a secret we shared knowing not everyone would understand. My gammy was our family fireball.

She, Jackson, and I had this internal live wire in us that never went off.

After Jackson left us, Gammy and I had been forced to close off a part of our fire. Mama had demanded it. We followed my mama's wishes because we thought it was the only way she could survive.

In the dark, I reached for my coffee-cup-print robe. As I threaded my arms into it, I crept into my son Wit's bedroom. My six-year-old replica of my brother slept peacefully.

I leaned over and planted a quiet kiss on his cheek. Tripod looked on with approval and followed me out.

I opened the back screen door, listening for the familiar screech of the spring and slam of wood.

As the cool air hit my body, I crossed my arms. The moon was a glorious sight as it made dancing reflections on the salt water. I walked across the cold grass until I could feel the refuge of the wooden plank underneath my feet.

Cleeve was still sitting up in the darkness, watching the silhouette of me and the deformed dog as we made our way down the dock.

I looked back at my quiet house and thought of my husband and son inside. I have always been proud of our old home. Don't think I am bragging, because I am not.

It's not new or artsy, but it's a family heirloom of sorts. I inherited it from the Churchill side of the family. It was supposed to have been Uncle Taft's house. You know, the one next to the Baileys' that I mentioned before? After Jackson died, Taft never wanted to live in Culley again. Gammy often said that it changed him in many ways. Naturally, everyone seemed to attach Jackson's death to the reason Taft had never married. We all knew that it was more than that, but it was another one of our hush zones.

He had given the home to me in memory of Jackson. Gammy and Pee-Paw had been just as proud that the house was mine as they were that Uncle Taft was so thoughtful in the name of our family.

The night Uncle Taft announced his decision about the house, Gammy hosted one of her big fish fries.

The family's hope was that I would never leave Culley since Mama and Daddy had lost one child already. I knew this, but we never spoke about it. Lots of things were never spoken of after Jackson left.

Our house had belonged to my great-grandparents. They were one of the Culley Cove Original Eight or TO8. Those very forefathers and mothers had cleverly designed the small beach community around the shape of the number eight.

This represented the team of families that had started the project after that Uncle Fiddler Churchill's sewage incident I mentioned before.

I am granddaughter to Mavis and Buckley Churchill. As you have noticed, I call them Gammy and Pee-Paw. They are to me the most perfect version of people that God ever made, next to our son, Wit, of course.

Our old home had become a sanctuary for me to write my stories, deal with my never-ending guilt, and raise our son, Wit. The house was family history while offering a warm place to hide from the world. Later, thanks to my gammy, it became the place where I took back freedom from fear.

The entire Churchill family had helped Cleeve and me renovate this old place. Generally, this meant that Gammy had directed everybody to do so. The Churchills made a point to listen to Gammy out of respect, loyalty, or just good ol' fear of the switch. Yes, even today Gammy can be known for popping her grown sons when she feels they need it.

I still love thinking back on those days of fixing up this old house. It was truly the first time my daddy and mama had laughed since Jackson's departure. Each of us continued to struggle every day trying to put it behind us. My moving forward, marrying Cleeve then taking over my great-grandparents' home seemed to give everyone some positive energy. It certainly didn't hurt that I was pregnant.

It also bookmarked the first time Uncle Taft had stayed in Culley for more than a week since he graduated from college. To be truthful, it was his first extended visit since Jackson left us.

My pee-paw had his Gospel music playing loudly from his red pickup truck. He parked it in our front yard while they worked.

He and Uncle Skeeter hung white bench swings from the massive oak trees in the center of our driveway. Gammy directed them on every inch they should move them before locking them into place.

I can still remember Uncle Skeeter getting fed up and saying, "I've just about had it, Mama. Make up your mind."

"Skeeter Churchill, you hush and do what I tell you! Do you hear me? If not, go find a switch for me and I will remind you, son," Gammy shot back at her then forty-seven-year-old son.

Daddy, Cleeve, and Uncle Taft had carefully resurrected the enormous wraparound porch, replicating the one my great-grandparents once had on the house.

Through the entire three-month process, Gammy, Mama and Nita had the smells of fried fish and swamp cabbage or chicken and dumplings pumping out through the windows. Nita had stuck by me throughout the ordeal with Jackson. She dated frequently, but never married. Gammy always said it was because she was so pencil thin. It was gammy's firm belief that there was something wrong with skinny women. If a female didn't like to eat she most likely didn't know how to cook. That was unacceptable according to gammy. We all loved Nita Ledbetter because she seemed to have a need for our family. There was something in my friend that was always lost. She was certainly one of the least selfish people I had ever known.

A number of our Baptist men would help on the weekends and then announce the newest developments on our house during Sunday service. I could feel some of the jealousy from the other members after awhile. I asked Pastor Caldwell to stop for that reason, only to find him doing a sermon on the likeness of our community to Jesus since he too was a carpenter. I decided from that minute on that God would have to decide how the jealousy played out in the church.

The final embellishment for my home came to fruition when my precious Pee-Paw showed up one day followed by two lumber trucks. The loud *beeps* from the trucks had drawn my attention outside.

"Granddaughter, I'm here to construct you a water dock," he said, smiling.

"Now, don't you say a word," he continued. "When my mama had this house, she had one. There wasn't a day that passed that I didn't see that poor old *thang* walk out there and sit in silence when she could steal it."

Pee-Paw could see it in his memory. He stopped, and I waited for him to savor that thought.

"There were times that she would just jump off it in her clothes and swim to shore," Pee-Paw said.

"She said it made her feel young and brave again. Why, my daddy almost committed her to Chattahoochee until he started joining her in the jumps," he explained.

Pee-Paw giggled to himself for a moment.

"I believe that may just be how my baby brother, Otus, was conceived," Pee-Paw would always add with a grin.

"Somehow the dock helped my old mama deal with all of us crazy Churchill boys," he continued. "She had eight of us, you know?

"Caroline, we love you and I know you must know it. Your brother had a mission when he was here and that was to bring us all together. He understood you from the minute you were born. Why, you could cry and that young man would walk over and pick you up and there was an instant connection. He knew it, and it made him find his place."

Now, Pee-Paw looked out over the water as the wind was picking up. I followed his gaze in silence.

He continued in his slow voice. "My mama used to say she did her best thinking out on her old dock."

I knew that she had died there in a rocking chair Pee-Paw made for her. He was thinking about that and I knew it, but also knew that this was his part of the story to tell, not mine.

"They found her right out there that afternoon with a smile on her face, Bible in her hand, and shoes off her feet," he said.

He kept his stare on the water where she died.

"Granddaughter, I want to give you the same thinkin' dock as my mama had," Pee-Paw whispered.

"I only hope you will use it as much as she did. I believe you will because you, like her, hold many loud secrets in your heart."

I still remember his twinkling blue eyes as he said this to me so sincerely, looking at my then very pregnant belly.

Chapter 5

VEILED VISIONS
1978

I swear I can still hear Jackson screaming up the stairs to me that afternoon to hurry up so I wouldn't miss the party—his voice like strings I wish I could pull and stop time, bringing him back.

As I was running down the hall, I had noticed his bedroom door was open. I walked in, just soaking in that he was home again. It was then I noticed that a piece of notebook paper was sticking out of his top dresser drawer. I put my bags down, walked over to stick it back in. Looking back, I don't know why I did this but I have to assume that I thought Mama might see it and read it before tucking it in the drawer. Absentmindedly I plucked up my heavy bags and started jumping down the stairs. As I turned the corner, his face broke into a smile. He grabbed my huge firefly suitcase full of dolls, crickets, bug jars, pajamas, and some sparklers. Elvis was barking excitedly beside my feet.

Jackson shook his head in a teasing way as he grabbed my bag and heard the chirping crickets.

"Mama will beat your tail if she finds out you are taking live crickets to Mrs. Ledbetter's house," he warned. "You know her husband, Alfred Ledbetter, is a neat freak kind of guy," Jackson added in a fun voice.

"He isn't from Culley but married into us," he reminded me with a smile.

"I suspect that's why Ustus is kind of different from the rest of us. Nita is cool but Ustus?" He made a questioning face and crossed his eyes.

"OK, Jackson, I get it. Ustus is a weirdo and you don't like him." I had fired the irritating remark.

"Sister, I think Mrs. Ledbetter and your buddy Nita are the only normal ones in that house. You just go over there, stay out of trouble, and play with the girls, OK?" he said with his eyes rounded to exaggerate them.

"All right, Jackson! You are turning into a weirdo yourself, man." I giggled at him.

He put his left arm around me and carried my oversized bag with his right. I broke away from him when Mama called to me from the kitchen.

"Young lady, I know you are gonna come in here and give your mama a kiss and talk about your plans," she said as she sprinkled pepper on raw chicken breasts.

"Remember, if you need us tonight we will be at Gammy and Pee-Paw's for the fish fry from five thirty till about nine, I figure. If not there, we should be here. Suzie Ledbetter has all of our numbers in the church directory.

"You behave, Caroline Churchill, do you hear me?" Mama asked. "None, and I mean none, of that squealing and jumpin' around. No pranks or sneakin' out, young lady. Are you listenin'? Now, you know Mr. Ledbetter is a Yankee."

She now stared at me with our noses almost touching.

"He doesn't understand our Southern style. So you go easy on your long-winded stories, and don't you dare tell any of our personal business. You listenin' to me, Caroline?" Mama asked.

"Yes, Mama," I said in an aggravated tone.

"Excuse me, young lady?" she looked at me with her brows almost pointed in the center.

"Uhh ummm. Yes, ma'am," I corrected.

"Now, that is better," she said. "A kiss, please."

Mama leaned over and hugged me tightly, and then pulled me back to look into my eyes and hugged me again. "I love you, Caroline," she said with such sincerity that her eyes watered.

"I love you too, Mama," I said and kissed her on the cheek.

She noticed Jackson's amusement over our dramatic departure for a one-night sleepover when she pulled me in close to her mouth. Her lips were touching my left ear.

"Did you pack you at least two pairs of clean panties?" she whispered with such strength that it tickled my ear.

"*Mama!*" I screamed.

At that, I remember running over to Jackson as if to say, "Take me now," and he understood.

Mama shouted one last time, "Jackson, remember Uncle Taft's fish fry starts at five thirty at Gammy and Pee-Paw's. I know he will expect you to get there earlier and visit, okaaay?" she chirped.

"*Yes, Mama!*" Those were Jackson's last words on this earth to our mama.

As we walked out of that front door together laughing we never knew we were being watched by a merciless soul. We never even felt it.

Daddy had retreated to his boat shed. I started running toward him for a good-bye hug. He gave a proud laugh and lifted me with his greasy hands. Mama would have required him to wash them before touching my clean clothes. We knew this and somehow all enjoyed the risk.

Daddy and Jackson discussed something about the engine, and Jackson walked over to look at it. We started our journey down the nature trail that curved along the coast.

Daddy had stopped and seemed to watch us walk away.

I remember Daddy yelled to Jackson, "Don't forget my brother's fish fry at Gammy's, son!"

You see, everybody reminded Jackson about things because he would get spacey sometimes. He was spontaneous and impulsive. The reminders seemed to help, according to Mama. This would be the last reminder from my daddy

Daddy says that generally he would have gone right back to working on his boat motor, but for some reason, that particular day he just leaned against the boat and watched us walking away. He recalls our slow steps and the giggling sounds as we walked down the nature trail together. This natural experience had been taken for granted up until this day. The next few days would challenge his strength in every way. He would be faced with the most difficult task a father can have, which is that of holding a broken family together.

* * *

In the thick of the woods, he entertained himself with his demented thoughts. As he stalked his prey, he noted all of his observations with obsessive detail. There was no need to write them down because he could remember every single morsel. He observed the interactions of others in order to emulate them with perfection for his sinister games. For him, human attachment was not a possibility.

Empathy was a characteristic that fascinated him because he was incapable of experiencing it. After all, his intellect had separated him from other foolish children. His pedantic father had told him that since he was old enough to understand English. His capacity to comprehend and apply knowledge was born of gifted intellect.

He had grown used to others finding him attractive because his good looks were undeniable. Even the perfect dark hair, tall muscular body and piercing blue eyes couldn't repair the damage done to him during childhood.

It had not been necessary for them to bond after his mother died. He was a dweller in the oversized mansion with his father who rarely spoke to him without criticism. The help would feed him and see to his physical needs. His father discouraged them from spending any social time with him because he didn't find it important.

He had learned from a young age to observe with perfection. He considered it a challenge to hone in on even the most inconsequential detail only to replay it in his mind later. It was a lesson of study for him. He would act in front of his mirror in his lonely room. He knew four languages fluently and could quickly jump from a southern accent articulating the differences between Texas and Tennessee in a second. He was never given an appropriate setting to try them out except in his fantasy world.

The home schooling teachers his father hired came and left quickly as they sensed an evil oddity about the boy after spending any substantial time with him. The only exception had been his first music teacher. Music was the only joy he was allowed. Even that came with a strict set of rules. It must always be classical. Whenever he tried to share his music with his father, hoping for praise, he was cut off by criticism for the slightest imperfections. Celia had been the one music instructor that had told him how talented he was. She even smiled while he played his instruments.

Later, she wanted to make his music more interesting and brought a guitar over for him one evening. This had been the only time in his life that someone had done something kind for him out of her own heart rather than being paid by his father. Once his dad recognized that he was actually enjoying the guitar he fired the teacher. He waited until dinner was served that evening to tell him that the teacher was gone. He had a huge fire burning in the dining room fireplace. Once dinner began, his father rose to grab the guitar from the buffet. He grabbed it and threw it into the fire. He wanted to torture his son by making him watch it burn. As they listened to the pops and cracks of the fire destroying the instrument, his father had looked up at him and simply said, "Sit up straight when dining."

Chapter 6

LOST MEMORIES
1978

The nature trail Jackson and I took was one we had walked all of our lives. It wound around behind almost every house on Culley Cove. The Ledbetter home was at the far end of the footpath. We playfully chased after the fiddler crabs in the sand that afternoon.

Whenever Jackson caught one, he pretended that he was going to eat it alive to tease me. I would scream, and he would throw it back onto the sand.

We walked behind what is now my home. Jackson reminded me that Uncle Taft would live there someday. After all, that is what we thought at that time. I remember his feet in the sand. I remember my hair ribbon that day. I remember the sounds of my junk clanking in the suitcase as Jackson walked. It's funny how the mind works. That day I can tell you so many minute details; however, I can't tell you an entire chunk of an important part.

The next part of my story was irretrievable for over two decades. It sat in my head like a TV screen when the power was out-Nothing. I continued to cast my line out there, but honestly, I was always relieved when I reeled in an empty hook. I couldn't remember it completely; yet, somehow I knew it was too dark for me to. I believe it's the mind's way of protecting us until we are ready.

My memory clicks straight into a perception I had about Jackson's behavior. He started acting rushed and nervous. I knew him well enough to know that he was covering something from me. I never knew what. Jackson always wanted me to think everything was OK.

"I sure hope Taft doesn't change too much while he is in college," Jackson said, kicking at the sand underneath his feet.

"Taft will never change," I said defensively.

"Caroline, Taft is different and you better not ever say that to mama or daddy. It doesn't mean he's a bad person. He just has to sort it out."

"Don't let other people tell you to be somebody you aren't, OK?" Jackson said so seriously.

He was rarely that severe with me. "Somebody messin' with you, Jackson?" I asked curiously.

"Lord no, girl. I just worry that someone will try to mess with you one day. Taft says crazy stuff goes on at college. I'm all about free love or whatever it is they all call it, but at the end of the day I want to come back to Culley and eat some of Gammy's fried catfish. Don't ever let anything happen to you that you are ashamed of, princess, OK?"

"You are starting to think everybody's weird, Jackson! I swear," I shouted, smiling at him.

"You know Pastor Smitty Caldwell says that when you point a finger at somebody, be careful 'cause you got three of 'em pointing back at you!" I reminded him.

"Good Lord, I see Mama has had you in serious training since I've been away," Jackson teased me. "That means I have some major work to do now that I'm home."

Then, we walked behind the Baileys' place. We heard Mr. Bailey's birddogs going nuts as we trailed by. Jackson considered stopping but saw my anxiousness about the party. He told me he would check in on the way back.

We enjoyed our time together until we finally approached the Ledbetter home. It was one of the more stately homes in Culley. Mrs. Ledbetter's grandfather was one of the Original 8.

She had rights to build on the property. Her husband, Mr. Ledbetter, was quiet and seemed to want to keep it that way. He didn't attend church services or school events.

You see, when you move into a small town like Culley and don't get to know everybody pretty fast, they suspect you have secrets. When you have too many of those and aren't willing to share them, people here assume you are full of trouble. That was the case with Alfred Ledbetter. He had waited too long to make any friends. Poor ol' Suzie was trying to make everybody believe he was too busy with his important job in the city. She created her little pocket of magical thinking in her head and tried to make everyone buy into it.

"Alfred is a delightful man," she once said at a revival retreat.

I heard Gammy whisper under her breath to Pee-Paw, "My ass."

Pee-Paw had shushed her quickly.

That morning, he was nowhere to be found. Most of the Culley Cove men got very involved with their children's events, with the exception of Mr. Ledbetter. He was a Yankee and a Catholic, so we figured this is what you got.

As we got closer to the Ledbetter home, we could hear the tribe of little girls squealing as they ran to greet me. I had arrived.

I was finally at Nita Ledbetter's stupid party that I wish I had skipped. If I had, maybe, just maybe, my brother would still be here today.

Poor ol' Ustus was out front dutifully trying to help his mama calm us girls down. I watched as he and Jackson spoke for a moment. Then, Jackson walked over to me and planted a kiss on the top of my head.

Then he leaned over to me and teased, "Yes, tell Mama I was nice to the weirdo. I just invited him to go fishin' with me later. You behave now, Caroline; always be true to yourself," he whispered as he hugged me for the last time before retreating to the saw grass walking trail.

That was the last time I would be with my brother on this earth. I saw him turn down the trail, but I never saw him walk to the corner nook of it. I had selfishly started playing a chase game with the other girls.

Chapter 7

NITA LEDBETTER'S PARTY
1978

That birthday party was as much fun as I had expected. The Ledbetters had won a big lawsuit in '72 over a car accident involving Suzie's mama. They had plenty of money, and Mr. Ledbetter commuted five days a week to the city, where he claimed to practice some sort of experimental medical treatment for underprivileged kids. None of us ever understood what it was, nor did we particularly care.

I don't remember seeing Ustus again until later that afternoon. As odd as Jackson had claimed he was, he had played with us and seemed eager to help his mama. Once you got past his zits that needed squeezing, I kind of thought he was OK. I felt sorry for him because he just didn't seem comfortable in his own skin.

I felt even worse for him when I walked inside to get another bowl of chips from the kitchen.

It was there that I found out poor Ustus was just mistreated. I heard Mr. Ledbetter's raised voice from the hallway. When I rounded the corner to the kitchen, I heard him calling Ustus a worthless no-good without direction. I saw him hit Ustus across the face. I turned and tiptoed down that hallway back out into the yard.

When I returned to the yard without the chips, Mrs. Ledbetter questioned me and I suppose read my face. She seemed to know what I had seen, which I suspect was all too familiar in her home. She rushed past me and ran inside. I didn't see her again for at least forty-five minutes.

* * *

Daddy says he continued working on his boat for hours, starting and stopping the engine to listen as he adjusted parts. Later, he fell asleep on the couch, watching an outdoor fishing show.

Mama remembers every detail of her afternoon. She says she walked over to Culley Baptist to practice her organ music until two o'clock. On her walk home, she stopped by to check in on her mother-in-law, my gammy.

Mama Shug and Gammy sat and had a cup of coffee together on the porch. They checked last-minute plans for the fish fry.

"Taft should be here any minute," Gammy said with the excitement of a child on Christmas morning.

"I reckon Jackson will be down here soon too," she said, almost questioning Mama. "I do declare I love listening to those two *young'ins* tell some of their new Churchill stories," she said as she banged the table, sloshing the coffee in the cups.

"I swear, Gammy, I see where my children got their high spirits," Mama said while patting the leg of her pants down, rising above the behavior.

"Praise the Lord, Rachel Churchill!" Gammy yelled out Mama's birth certificate name.

Mama and Gammy were mother and daughter-in-law, but just as close as if they were blood because they shared blood. They had a mutual, unspoken respect for one another. Their allegiance had been built since Mama Shug's birth. My mama had been an only child whose mother died during childbirth. My Gammy had been Mama's mother's best friend. Gammy took mama under her wing and helped my grandfather raise her until his death when mama was only fourteen years old.

Gammy saw her opportunity to defend her coffee slosh.

"I do take pride in what these crazies call *hyper*," Gammy ranted.

"I consider it a life skill," she said loudly. "I figure they get it from me. Can you imagine if everybody in this old world made us all out to act like Alfred Ledbetter? That medicine-maker, or whatever he is, with his uptown job. None of us even understands what it is he does. Why, we would sleep all day from sheer boredom," she said rounding her eyes like large marbles.

Gammy took a slurp of her coffee and added another sugar packet to it before starting up again.

"I love my offspring kickin' up the dust. They make this place interestin'," Gammy continued in her evangelistic voice.

The women fell back into conversation as gently as they started. Gammy asked if Jackson mentioned Taft teaching some of the classes at the revival camp. She was digging to hear about her youngest son's talent at teaching scripture. Gammy was always reaching for the reasons her youngest child was somewhat different. Her summary on the subject was always the same, "My Taft is different, but he is mine and I love him."

The two women shared how fortunate they were to have the Lord and this fine family. These details of their day would be something that would haunt them forever. At this very moment, a hellish soul had taken one of their own as they sat enjoying their afternoon coffee.

Around four thirty that afternoon, Mama says she and Daddy met back at home to clean up for Gammy and Pee-Paw's fish fry. It was then that Mama asked if Jackson was home yet.

Daddy brushed it off with one of his "boys will be boys" speeches. Mama recalls showering as she forced off her irritation about Jackson's tardiness. She slipped her jeans on accompanied by a pink and cream striped oxford. She wore her simple pearls bequeathed to her by her father. She fussed about getting them to sit just right inside her collar.

Around five o'clock, just before she and Daddy started over to Gammy and Pee-Paw's, Mama called the Ledbetter house to check on me. She asked Suzie Ledbetter when Jackson had left their house. Suzie confirmed it had been hours ago. Then, as an afterthought, she mentioned that her son, Ustus, told her that a group of the boys were meeting at the marina to go fishing.

Mama remembers she and Daddy had stopped by the Baileys' house to see if maybe Jackson had gotten tied up looking after their brood of dogs. Daddy rang the bell and then got the key from under the kitchen windowsill to enter. Mama says she had stomach cramps while daddy was in the house looking around. She was unsettled and couldn't make her mind overpower her body from the tenseness she felt.

Daddy inspected the house deciding it looked clean, noting the lights that were on the day before had been switched off and others were now on. This was what Jackson was supposed to do to make it look as if the Bailey's were home, scaring off the toilet paper bandits. Their dogs had fresh food and water.

As Daddy approached the car, he yelled out to Mama, "I told you everything was just fine. The lights have been changed and all dogs are happy as can be."

"Titus, I don't feel good about this. I can't explain it," Mama had said while staring out of the car window. Daddy noticed her facial expression mirroring one he remembered from when she was so young and her daddy had died. He reached his right hand over to find hers.

"Sugar, you just haven't raised a boy before. I thought Jackson had trained you by now," he said laughing.

"Now, let's go eat fish!"

Chapter 8

THE FISH BEGIN TO FRY
1978

So the fish fry started that evening without Jackson. Daddy says Uncle Taft made his way around the crowd to visit everyone. He was thanking them for coming. His concern about Jackson's absence was obvious to everyone. Historically, the two boys were the life of the party with their dramatic stories.

Each time there was a sound outside, daddy says Gammy would go look for Jackson, turning back, shaking her head no, and then glancing at Mama.

At first, Gammy agreed that Jackson was probably absentminded and would be there any minute. She reminded my mama about all of the boys she raised and how they never ceased to amaze her.

As my mama dipped the mullet from the egg butter mixture to the corn meal to the hot grease, she says she knew something wasn't right. "Mothers always know," she had said every day since that one.

Mama remembers that she called the Ledbetter house again to ask more about this fishing trip. Her mind raced with thoughts of her conversation with Jackson that morning. *He would have never gone off with Ustus*, she thought. Then she concluded that maybe her harsh Christian judgment that morning had encouraged Jackson to be overly kind to Ustus. Suzie Ledbetter put her son on the phone with Mama Shug and he could not materialize the names of the boys that were planning the fishing trip.

Just before supper, Daddy and Skeeter decided to ride around the beach to look for Jackson. They did this more to shut Gammy and Mama up than anything else. After all, what could happen to anybody at Culley Cove when you knew every rock and stick on the island?

Gammy says she hesitated on serving the cakes and coffee before Jackson arrived, but finally had no choice.

It was at nine- thirty that Gammy says she stood up from her bench swing. She raised her voice in military tone. "I have had enough!" she yelled.

"I am calling the First Baptist Church of Culley and we are finding my grandbaby. Churchills, get going!" she ordered.

When Gammy talked, everybody listened. It was then that brothers, cousins, and friends were put on alert. The men communicated on their CB radios as they did during hunting season. Trucks were moving over the island with their extended antennas flappin' in the wind. The silence of the night was cut with the calling of my brother's name.

Daddy recalls the church kitchen was opened, and the ladies began cooking and setting up coffee stations. Suzie Ledbetter had been contacted to assist. She called Mama and told her she would start some meals, even with the girls sleeping over. She went on to say her husband, Alfred, wanted to help with the search.

Pastor Caldwell and his wife, Toot, showed up within ten minutes of Gammy's call. He explained that his son, Landen, drove the Baptist revival van on Friday. He had stated that he had driven Jackson home late Friday evening. Mama looked over and shook her head in agreement.

"Yeah, you got him to us just fine, Pastor," Mama explained. "It was after we got him that we didn't watch him well enough," she said, looking shameful.

"Now, Sister Sugar," Pastor said, "there is no need to blame yourself."

"Your affection for your children is obvious to us all," Pastor continued. "Don't let that nasty devil get up in your head and taunt you," he said as his voice rose.

Then Pastor Caldwell did the only thing that he could at that moment. He stood in Gammy's living room asking everyone to join hands.

He started the Lord's Prayer. "Our Father who art in heaven..." And the prayer was completed and followed by specific prayers for Jackson's safe return home.

At this, Mama had started crying as she fell into Pee-Paw's chair. Gammy walked over to her and ordered her up. She told Mama that this was not the time. Mama's daddy died when she was so young. Gammy was always the anchor during crisis and Mama knew it. Jackson needed us and we had work to do. Mama needed the support and strength, and up she went.

In her heart, Mama always says she knew that she wouldn't see Jackson again. Looking back, it was telling in her behavior from the start. Somehow it was different from everyone else's consciousness. The irony of it was that my mama would be the first to know, but the last to accept.

Mama had started developing her coping mechanism about Jackson at that moment. The doctors had a fancy name for it, but we broke it down in terms we Churchills could understand. She somehow knew she would not have the ability to face this cruel reality. For her, hiding behind her own delusions would somehow keep him alive in her mind.

Chapter 9

THE SEARCH BEGINS
1978

The Culley men were checking out the boat-houses, marina boats, and vacated buildings. They looked at each boat that was transported across the bridge from the service shop to the big marina.

Daddy and his brothers recalled they were in their airboats. Each airboat had two Q beams shining in the marshes while the captains would steer. I remember the searches that went on for days. In my mind I can still hear the men yelling to one another about anything at all that they found in or near the water. It was assumed that he had hurt himself walking down the nature trail or decided to wade in the marsh, looking for baitfish.

Pee-Paw said the Culley police, as well as police from some of the surrounding counties, were helping in the search. At that point, no one was certain on which beach Jackson may be found. Word was spreading quickly. Reports had come in that Jackson had been sighted in various areas near Culley. All of these leads turned out to be a hopeful person seeing someone with a red shirt and longer brown hair. Still, it was assumed that there was a mishap with a boat somewhere, as was usually the case when anyone in our area couldn't be found right away.

Mama, accompanied by Gammy, decided to drive over to the Ledbetters' sleepover that evening. My mama needed to see me and just hug the one child she could find at the moment.

For the first time since he had lived in Culley, Alfred Ledbetter walked over and actually had a conversation with Mama and Gammy. He seemed so sympathetic about something with Mama. I watched them talking and tried not to appear to be surprised. He had offered to help in any way he could, Mama explained to me later. He asked them questions and seemed to absorb the news inside the pores of his skin. In moments, he disappeared with his unusually casual clothing to join the search.

I knew nothing of my brother's situation at that time, which still angers me somewhat. I sat there in my frilly pajamas like a fool, eating popcorn and giggling with little girls while my brother was lost forever. I know that my family was trying to sort out the details and solve the problem in hopes of sparing me the fear.

I remember noticing Mama hug Suzie Ledbetter before she left. I knew that was highly unusual.

My brain was trying to imagine reasons for Mama and Suzie to be so friendly. I had pieced together a mangled summary that some small crisis must have taken place at the church. Maybe one of the old ladies had a cold and couldn't make her pie for the Sunday revival.

* * *

He was impatiently waiting for news of the missing boy. Perhaps it would be in the papers or on the television the next day. His crazed mind anticipated the small-minded reactions. He had watched these people as if they were lab rats in order to make his predictions.

His father had shown him the importance of strategy. His father had taught him that much in life. He pointed his long, wicked finger to the wrong people in an effort to confuse.

Manipulating others came as easily for him as drinking water. He had learned how to bribe the house help, engineering his plans from a young age. Money was plentiful in that house and he had learned over time how to extract it from the old man and use it to get what he needed. The world was there for his taking. He was damaged.

He started singing in a tiny, slightly demonic voice.
"Where is Jackson?
Where is Jackson?
Have you found him yet?"

Chapter 10

MAMA SHUG'S DELUSION
2001

Mama Shug's Lincoln slowly makes its way down our driveway each morning to take my son, Wit, to school. She shows up promptly at 7:15 a.m., honking that damn horn. We are in rhythm with the same actions every day. I walk out on the porch and wave while she slurps her coffee. Then she sends her passenger window down, dispensing fumes of White Linen, giving battle against the salty air.

Today, Mama knew that I had one of my appointments. She, Daddy, Gammy, and Pee-Paw always keep track of my doctor appointments. Each of them needed therapy; however, I was the only one who actually believed in such measures.

We didn't refer to him as the *psychologist* or *head doctor* or even *shrink*. It was more of the way we said it than what we called it. Mama leaned her Aqua Net hairsprayed hair over, grazing the ceiling of the car. In a raspy whisper, she asked. "Are you going to meet with the *doctor* this morning?" The word *doctor* she said with a slow, raspy whisper.

"Yes, Mama," I said. "Don't you want to come along and meet with him too?" I asked sarcastically.

Now, her brows were in a Jack Nicholson point. "Caroline Churchill Burton, I will not entertain your nasty words this mornin'. I'll have you know that according to our Culley Ladies Prayer Group, I have dealt well with the loss of my child."

"You keep believin' that, Mama," I said, taking an intended long sip of my coffee.

Her finger had just come up and her lips were pursed for some profound comment as little Wit barreled out of the front door.

"*Morning*, Gammy Shug!" he said, excitedly jumping down the steps with his lunchbox in hand.

"Oh, there's my boy. Come here and give Gammy Shug some sugar," she cheered, clapping her hands together.

"Wit, I swear, you look like you grew from last night to today," she said. "You get more and more handsome every day, dear."

Mama sang these words as she accelerated on the gas pedal. She and Wit slowly exited the graded drive at a turtle's pace. It took her forever to gain speed since Daddy had once told Mama that she could rip the engine out of the car if she drove too fast on a graded road.

I always think of the form of Mama's teased head turning this way and that as she talked to Wit.

You see, my Wit had become everyone's surrogate for Jackson. Perhaps this was even the case with me in some ways. They shared an uncanny resemblance, but then again, Jackson and I looked very much alike.

He certainly had the same hyperactivity issue that my brother and I shared. Mama and Daddy never wanted to hear about it.

After Mama's constant warnings to Jackson to calm down, she seemed to actually celebrate Wit's need to explore and raise his voice. It was almost as if she found Jackson inside of Wit. She was going to hold on to both of them like nothing she had held on to before.

You have to understand that my mama had been told many times about the five stages of grief. Her nerve pills helped her park in the denial and isolation stage for a few years. Then somehow, she managed to skip all of the other stages of grieving, moving straight into number five. This was the acceptance stage of grief. She accepted that Jackson was gone, but she never accepted how he left this earthly world.

My mama had created her very own coping mechanism after my brother's death. You see, she made up a delusional world regarding Jackson's death, so that she never had to think of him suffering. She decided that

Jackson had died in his sleep. She would never listen to anything else, no matter how concrete the evidence.

Mama had found Jackson again in my Wit. I sometimes used to wonder, before she got better, if she ever truly believed that he wasn't Jackson.

I jolted myself back into reality as I noticed the car had finally made its way out of the drive with the engine intact. There was no doubt: Wit and Mama were headed for Poppell's Bakery. That would sugar him up right before school. I would likely get my school notification that afternoon.

No one would listen to me, though; as long as Wit was showered with everything he wanted, our Churchill family seemed to feel validated. We were doing it for Wit and Jackson.

Chapter 11

MEETING WITH MY HEADDOCTOR
2001

My appointment was at ten o'clock in the city. I had just enough time to shower, dress, and make the hour long drive.

The waiting area of Dr. Chapman's office was decorated in an overstated formal style. Classical music played gently in the background. Regal draperies and tasteful furniture adorned the area around the secretary. It was obvious that this superficial decadency made her feel important. She took her job so seriously that it amused me. Her refusal to make conversations with the patients was deliberate as were her mannerisms. Her inappropriate use of verb tenses told me all that her staged performances tried to cover.

Doc's personal office was designed in stark contrast to the waiting room. His domain was done in tranquil colors. The theme was extremely eclectic. Somehow it cleared my mind to be in there. Often I imagined his team of decorators presenting the ideas to him based on settling the nerves of his patients.

Doc typically had tea or coffee to offer in cups with positive sayings written on the sides in calligraphy.

Today my coffee mug had the words: *Time is precious, but truth is more precious than time.* This is precisely what ol' doc had been trying to drive through my thick head. He made it seem as if he had predicted the outcomes of my session long before my arrival.

Dr. Chapman was the 13th psychologist I had seen since 1980. He was stronger than the others and had a no nonsense approach. What I liked most about him was that he didn't let me control my sessions like I had done with all of the others. He steered me so that I could grab pieces of information that had been lost by my family's denial.

My refusal to follow the steps with so many of these types of doctors had often required a parting of ways. My therapy up until now was a game for me about sending the doctors on goose chases while I insulated my true pain with a protective coating. I am hard headed and also in quite an odd situation with my family.

I found myself mentally preparing for my session. An inner conflict began to rise and shake me. The reason for this was unclear but always present.

Half an hour later, I lay on the sofa in Dr. Chapman's office. There was no doubt his peppering questions were about to begin.

Dr. Chapman was an older man who had a sophisticated appearance. He didn't wear a wedding ring, but he may have been the type that felt that you didn't need symbols like that. I often imagined how he handled his personal life after giving advice to others most of the week. He wasn't handsome but intriguing in an intellectually odd sort of way. He typically pulled his round glasses to the end of his nose while waiting for my answers. His wiry fingers were always accessorized with a pen spontaneously jotting notes in his folder.

"Caroline, how does it make you feel when you jump off your dock?" he asked while adjusting the tassel on his dress shoe.

"Alive!" I said quickly.

"I feel like I did before Jackson left us. I can conquer the world. I can make noise. I can be daring. I believe it's who I would have been if..." I stopped.

"Continue", he said in a slightly arrogant tone.

Silence.

"Caroline, I feel that it's very therapeutic for you to have found this outlet. It is indeed healthy. This jumping is your way of battling your inner conflict," Doc Chapman continued.

"Now, can you tell me about your nightmares during the last week?"

I lay there in silence as my mind changed the channels quickly searching for the memory that may send him down a diversion adventure as opposed to that of my true fears.

It was then that I started thinking about how strange therapy was to me. You go because you know you need help. Now, I didn't say I was crazy, but just needed to sort out my reasoning.

You want the poor ol' doc to help you, but you get ticked off when he asks you questions. My knee-jerk reaction was, "It's none of your damn business!"

Then, I realized that not only had I driven my happy ass there to talk, but also was paying for the service. It was confusing.

Doc started. "If you are unwilling to share them with me in the privacy of this office, I can't begin to help them go away."

There was Doc's dismissal of me again. He had an uncanny way of making me feel as if I could leave at any time. He didn't need me. For some strange reason that had become precisely why I continued to see old Doc Chapman.

Suddenly, I could hear my voice begin, seemingly without my approval.

"Jackson and I were walking down the trail that day on our way to Nita's party," I recalled.

"We were laughing and teasing each other like we always did. As we approached the Baileys' house we heard their dogs. They were barking like crazy. Jackson wanted to feed them, but I was rushing him because of the party. He dismissed it and told me he would come back and do it."

"Sometimes I think someone was there," I said honestly about my confusion.

Doc and I both knew I hadn't shared this before.

"Who do you see, Caroline?" Doc probed.

"No one," I said. "It's just something in nightmares."

"What does the person look like in your nightmares?" Doc dug deeper.

"He is about Jackson's age," I explained. "He might be older than him, but not by much.

"It isn't real, though," I repeated, looking over at Doc Chapman.

"I can still hear those searchers calling out Jackson's name," I intentionally diverted the conversation. "They were yelling all over the island."

"This comes up each time we discuss that night and the days that followed. Why do you think the sounds of the searchers calling Jackson's name bothers you so much?" He asked.

"I don't know exactly, but it does," I explained. "Maybe it's because their call to him and his not responding was the reality. He would never respond."

"I think that is a very good way of putting it," Doc agreed. "You seem to have a grasp on why you are still unsettled by his death. You understand that you are coping instead of completely accepting. There are naturally many reasons for this.

"There is a great deal of conflict inside of your mind," he said.

Doc knew from previous sessions that mama had her own issues about Jackson. You see, she made up a delusional world regarding it so that she never had to think of the horrible details. She wouldn't listen to anything else, no matter how concrete the evidence may be.

Again, I paused to hold back the tears. This damn weakness in me that I hated continued to accompany me to these sessions. I couldn't escape it.

"I see from your childhood documents your parents noted your struggles with hyperactivity, anxiety and grief. Naturally, your father has provided most of it since your mother was unable to discuss it."

There was silence. I wasn't taking the bait to pounce on my mother.

Doc Chapman tugged once more," One of the items from your mother's questionnaire mentions you waking up as a child screaming about Jackson.

You were warning him to be careful of the man. What man do you see in your nightmares, Caroline?"

I looked at him angrily and asked, "Does Mama also have in my notes that she requires us all to pretend Jackson died in his sleep?"

Then I huffed for a moment like a child. This was the part of therapy that amused me. It was acceptable to act as crazy as a cricket in a hubcap and no one could say a word. Thank the good Lord for patient privacy laws. We were one of the few families that had good insurance to pay head doctors. I figured Doc wouldn't want me committed since that would stop my visits.

"Caroline, we have discussed why your mother needed to retreat from reality. As for you, perhaps you needed to cope with the truth of the incident," he added.

"I have listened to my mama tell us all how we should just picture Jackson asleep on that big old rock," I said sarcastically.

"He just fell asleep and died peacefully," Mama repeats as if it's the gospel. When we challenge her we have to listen to her sermon about how the old devil is eatin' up our brain by the tablespoon."

Doc was aware of the disruption mama's fantasies about Jackson had been on my childhood. The school finally required me to go to therapy. They realized that Mama wasn't dealing with the reality of our loss in a healthy way. Daddy had to sign the releases to allow it.

Doc sat quietly for a moment in deep thought before speaking.

I was certain in his head doctor symposium of thoughts I was a marvelous bug under the microscope ready for dissection.

"Children need an open atmosphere in dealing with death," he started reverting back to his condescending tone.

I couldn't respond. I hated the weakness that took charge of my body whenever I reached deep into my soul about Jackson.

"You should have been told that there was no one way to feel. There is not a right or wrong way to deal with your thoughts about death. It's a process, and the way you handle it should change. You were told how to grieve and forced to believe something that you knew wasn't accurate. If you challenged it, you feared harming your mother's welfare.

"In your family, all of you shared the common loss; each of you handled it differently. This is primarily because you all had your own unique relationship with Jackson. Your mother got so tangled in her own grieving process that she neglected to consider how it harmed those around her."

"Does that make sense?"

"Yes."

"Caroline, you were caught between grieving the loss of your brother and helping your mother stay whole. That's a heavy load for a young girl."

He let the room fall into silence again- which I interpreted as an intentional dramatic pause.

"Jackson was the only person you believed really understood you. You needed to grieve that loss as well as the tangible one."

"You are angry because your mother still won't allow the conversations about what happened. This anger is getting worse, not better with age; therefore, you need to do something about it. She can't stop you from investigating and learning about what really happened," he explained.

"You are a grown woman. You are not responsible for anyone else as an adult."

"I know," I said.

"You have created a virtual wall there that doesn't exist. She can't dictate how you handle Jackson's death anymore."

"Do you understand?"

I shook my head in agreement to appease him.

"Now, you don't have to include her in your explorations," he concluded. "You, however, can do what you need to do."

He continued, "Right this minute, how do you feel about your mother's choice to create her fantasy about your brother's death?"

"Well, I am angry; however, I understand," I said. "Please know that Mama did the best she could with it."

Now, Doc Chapman pointed his finger at me raising his voice, "See, right there you are protecting your mother as opposed to dealing with your own feelings!"

He was the only doc that had actually tried to get me angry.

"Caroline, I will not let you off the hook. I am here to push you into places you and your family have fenced out of reach," he said with a determined expression on his face.

Then the silence ensued as he glared at me.

"It's time to switch sandboxes," Caroline.

It was official at that moment that Doc Chapman was the one person that could get me to a new level. Certainly, I could never let him in on this epiphany.

"I am proud of mama for knowing her limits," I explained. "It takes guts to realize what you can handle and sometimes what you can't. I think she stopped herself from losing her mind, honestly."

"As for me, I needed the real stuff. I needed to face it. I am a fighter by nature, but I have been placed in a cotton cocoon and disallowed from being who I was meant to be."

"Is there anyone else in your family who allows that freedom for you, Caroline?" he asked.

In a single second, I said, "Gammy."

"She is a great deal like Jackson and me. Gammy encourages me to jump off the dock in my underwear," I said as Doc smiled back at me.

"It's good that you have your grandmother to bounce your thoughts off, and I hope you use that. She likely needs you for that same thing, huh?" he asked.

The room fell back into that staged pause that accentuated the rhythm of our conversation.

Finally, I found words to attach to my thoughts. I stared motionless at the ceiling and started explaining my mind to the best of my ability.

"Maybe, but Gammy doesn't like to ask anybody for anything. She is very independent."

"You realize that her not asking is not a direct sign that she doesn't need help at times?" he asked. "After all, you need to discuss Jackson's death, and you don't let anyone know that. Do you see the parallel? Perhaps your gammy struggles over this problem just as you do."

I sat quietly, thinking about Doc Chapman's words.

"My problem is that I'm afraid."

"Afraid of what?"

"I feel that I failed Jackson,"

"Why?"

"I can't remember details anymore" I said as my voice wobbled.

"What details?"

"I mean... I remember things that seem unimportant. I am afraid of what was done to Jackson. Did he suffer?" Was he conscious? I am sure I don't even know everything with all of mama's secrets."

"I'm the one who told him about Taft coming home that weekend," I explained. " I hoped it would make Jackson come back sooner."

"Do you still feel guilty about that?" He probed.

"Wouldn't you?" I snapped, wiping my eyes.

"Well, no, I wouldn't. He knew he was loved and you wanted him to come home. Don't you believe that made him feel happy?"

I didn't answer the stupid question.

"Caroline?"

Silence.

"It's important that you deal with the fact that you didn't cause this to happen," Doc said, sounding like a broken record. "It was out of your control."

My shrill cry started back, and I continued, "I made Jackson come home, and then he walked me to the Ledbetters' that day."

"Caroline, I understand how you feel, and you are correct that many of us feel guilt over many things," he explained. "Often, however, these are things we have no control over. Sometimes perhaps we could have altered our behavior to undo the situations somewhat. Don't you believe that the outcomes would still be the same?"

"Your brother was meant to leave this earth that day, Caroline. Nothing you could have done or not done was going to change that fact. You must begin to accept that after all of this time. You simply must," he said as he jotted a note in his little folder.

"There is something that I remember," I said slowly. "I often dream about it, and I never told Mama or Daddy."

"Yes," Dr. Chapman said, encouraging me to go on.

I opened my eyes and looked over at him. "This is confidential, isn't it?" I asked.

"Absolutely," he confirmed.

"It's nothing really."

"Continue, he said now leaning forward."

"The morning before Jackson and I walked over to the Ledbetters', I walked into his bedroom. There was a piece of notebook paper sticking out of his dresser drawer. Looking back, I must have been afraid for Jackson that Mama would read it. Anyway, I put it back into the drawer and closed it tightly. I forgot to mention it to Jackson later. In fact, I didn't even think about it until I got home the next day and found out that he was missing."

I reached over to get a sip of water, trying to collect my nervous thoughts before I could continue.

"Later, I went back and got the note in case, with him missing, Mama might nose through it again, you know?"

"Yes," he nudged me to continue.

"I went into my room and read it."

I paused.

"Continue."

"It was a letter to my Uncle Taft. "He and Jackson must have had some sort of argument over something. Jackson was apologizing."

"He was basically giving Uncle Taft advice to do something that he didn't want to."

I stopped and told Doc Chapman I couldn't go on anymore. I felt so physically and emotionally exhausted.

"Very good, Caroline," Dr. Chapman went on. "OK, let's not discuss the contents of the letter anymore today, but how about what you did with the letter? Who else read it?"

"Uncle Taft," I said.

"How did Uncle Taft react to it when you gave it to him?" Dr. Chapman asked me curiously.

I felt my face heat up as my defenses went into action.

I sat on the sofa and raised my voice to the doctor. "I don't think I like what you are implying."

"Why, I'm not implying anything, Caroline," he went on. "What is it you feel that I am saying?"

"Doc you think Uncle Taft hurt Jackson!"

"I think no such thing. Perhaps you feel a sense of guilt for showing the letter to your uncle," Doc said challenging me.

Again, I felt the sense of being a lab rat being tested.

"*No, no!*" I screamed. "Jackson told us that morning that he needed to apologize to Uncle Taft but he never went into any detail. This was his apology. It was one of the things he wanted to do that day. I was helping Jackson!"

I suddenly realized that the poor receptionist could likely hear all of my drama. I could only hope that she was familiar with that client confidentiality policy.

Then, I curled into a fetal position and bawled my eyes out. Doc Chapman sat down beside me and hugged me.

"Caroline is there a tiny piece of you that carries suspicion about your Uncle Taft's involvement in your brother's death?"

I didn't answer. I wouldn't answer. This was a thought only I was allowed to have and when it surfaced I threw it right back out like a sack of garbage. I would betray my family if I ever said it out loud.

I wouldn't answer him but he wanted me to contemplate his inference.

Doc then tapped my leg lightly and told me that our time was up.

"You are making progress, and there was a time I wasn't sure if you would," he said seriously. I see you breaking through walls that have needed to come down for such a long time. How quickly you move forward is up to you and what you are willing to share.

Chapter 12

BROKEN GLASS-BROKEN FAMILY
1978

I couldn't find sleep that night at my best friend's sleepover. Even though all of the girls had sworn they would stay up until morning, not one of them did. I remember being angry with them. I kept trying to wake them up but they would fall right back to sleep. I got up and walked into the kitchen as I often did at home. I got a glass of milk, knowing somehow that Mama wouldn't think that was proper. I took it out on the back porch and plopped down on a rocking chair. It was four in the morning and the moon was full. The rocker made bumping sounds on the wood porch as I rocked it. I remember feeling the beauty of the bright night but also something inside of me was unsettled.

Suddenly, car lights began coming up the driveway at the Ledbetter house. I saw that it was Mr. Ledbetter's old garden truck. He rarely used it except to take the trash to the dump. I was afraid he wouldn't think it was proper for me to have helped myself to their refrigerator for milk. I was so nervous that I jumped off the side of the porch. I crouched down behind the lattice. I was certain if I had run into the front door, he would have seen me. I tried to control my breathing the best I could. My hands were shaking and the milk was sloshing onto my pajamas. I found the courage to peep over the top of the porch floor to look. He was covered from head to toe with mud and marsh grass.

I had never seen Mr. Ledbetter in anything but a suit or dress clothes. I didn't even know he owned waders, but I guess he did. Even in my excitement my mind pictured Gammy finding humor in Ledbetter dressed like that.

As I was watching him, I forgot I was holding my glass of milk and dropped it. It tapped the edge of the porch and broke with a loud shatter. Shards of glass shot out across the porch and the side yard.

"Hello! Who's there?" he called out, looking around.

"Hello!" he called again.

I had only one thing to do and that was to confess to taking milk without permission.

"Oh, ah...hello, Mr. Ledbetter, sir," I said, timidly stumbling on my words. "I was thirsty and everyone was asleep," I started to explain.

Had this been my daddy, he would have laughed and assured me to get all of the milk I wanted. He would follow that by explaining how he and Mama hated those glasses. Breaking it was actually doing them a favor, he would say.

Mr. Ledbetter, however, grimaced at me as if I had burned the house down.

"Young lady, I do not know what the rules are in your home but here our children are not permitted to use glass for this very reason," he said as his voice was rising.

"How clumsy can you be, girl?" he yelled. "You go and drop a glass onto a porch? What are you doing out here, anyway? I specifically ordered Suzie to keep all of you brats inside Sonita's room for the evening.

This *Sonita* I had never heard, but later found out it was Nita's birth certificate name. Usually when somebody used those names, they were mad.

My lip began to quiver, followed by a wave of tears. No man had ever spoken to me that way. In our family, Gammy and Mama did the discipline. Daddy kind of reminded and reassured me when I messed up.

He then raised his hand, as Daddy did to his bird dogs, and yelled, "Shoo!"

I heard Suzie running onto the porch.

"What in the world?" she asked with excitement and dread.

At this, Alfred Ledbetter walked over to her and looked down at her with intimidation. "I told you not to let these brats come out of that room, Suzie."

He raised his hand to her as if he thought of hitting her, but stopped. Suzie started crying and begged him not to get angry because the girls were all in the house.

Then, he directed her stare to me. "There, see what that one did? She's out of the room and helped herself to our milk. Now she's broken a perfectly good piece of crystal," he yelled as he walked up the stairs of the porch.

It was then that Suzie came over to me and hugged me. Through her embarrassment, she must have seen my fear. Somewhere in her soul, I am sure she was afraid I might repeat it to Mama and Daddy at some point. She never said a word about that. It was at that moment that I knew Suzie Ledbetter was a good woman. She may talk too much at times, but she was trying to do the best she could. She had to live with this old mean-as-cuss husband of hers and I felt sorry for her.

She even told me not to worry about the glass. As she was cleaning the shards off the floor, she told me that Mr. Ledbetter had a hard life.

She said that he got angry over the simplest of things. She reassured me that he was a good man and meant no harm.

I remembered hearing Mama and Gammy say that Suzie's mom wanted her to marry Mr. Ledbetter 'cause he had money. I doubt she loved him. I couldn't help but think that Suzie and her mama should have just held out for the car accident money. Now poor Suzie was like my Aunt Sadie. They were stuck with mean men who would dictate their freedom and cage their spirit.

After Mrs. Ledbetter and I finished cleaning up the shards of glass I walked back upstairs. Quietly, I entered Nita's dark bedroom. The moon gently cast enough light for me to barley see my friends' sprinkled around the room in their sleeping bags.

My best friend status had given me the privilege of sleeping in the canopy bed with Nita. I slipped into the linens and turned over closing my eyes. Just as I was trying to forget the ugliness of what I had experienced, I heard Nita's sniffle.

"I'm so sorry, Caroline, she whispered into the darkness of the room.

"What for?" I decided to play dumb.

"I'm sorry for my daddy. I know he can be so scary but he promised mama he would be good for my party."

"It was ummm... my fault. I walked into the kitchen and got a fancy crystal glass and broke it."

"No, he gets too mad. Mama says he doesn't mean it. Sometimes he is as nice as can be. Mama says daddy had a bad home life."

"Nita, don't you worry about any of that one bit. You know how clumsy I am."

"My daddy isn't always nice like yours. You are so lucky to have the family you do."

"Come on Nita. We have our moments too."

"I love you Caroline. You're my best friend in the whole wide world."

We never discussed the events of that night again... Ever.

Chapter 13

MISSING
1978

The morning couldn't come soon enough for me. I was never happier to see my mama than that morning when she drove up to get me. I had been packed up and ready from the moment I went up to Nita's room after that incident.

Surprisingly, Mr. Ledbetter was sitting quietly at the kitchen table. He seemed eager to talk with Mama. He didn't mention a word about the night before. He was eager to explain to her that he had been out on a search. I did not know what this meant at the time. Mama shushed him and glanced at me. He seemed to honor her wish, which shocked me given his behavior toward Suzie the night before.

We said our good-byes, and I couldn't help but notice Mama seemed to be disheveled. She had not fixed her hair properly, and her pants seemed to have dirt smears on them. I knew better than to ask because Mama would have had a hissy fit.

Once we were sitting in her car, her eyes watered with tears. She swallowed hard and said, "Caroline, Daddy is waiting for us at Gammy and Pee-Paw's. We need to talk to you."

In my stupidity, I thought to myself that Mr. Ledbetter must have called them last night about my breaking the glass after all. Mama and Daddy were going to let me have it.

When we pulled into the driveway, there were cars parked all over. People were congregated on the porch. Boat trailers were lined up at Pee-Paw's boat ramp like a fishing tournament. Gammy grabbed me out of the car and hurried me inside. Pee-Paw put me beside him on the couch and held on to me.

Something told me that this was more than me getting milk and breaking a glass at the Ledbetter house. I could feel the tension in the air. I have often heard that expression, but that day I felt it.

Daddy squatted down in front of me and barely got out my name before he melted into tears. I will never forget that moment because until the next few days, it was the most horrible I had experienced. The strongest man I knew was on the floor, trying to speak, and started crying like a baby. Gammy walked over to Daddy. She started rubbing his back while whispering his name.

It was that moment that Pee-Paw looked over at me and we communicated through our eyes as we so often did. It was as if God took his sensible tongue and gave him the strength to put together words that I could understand.

"Sweet Caroline," he said, "Jackson is missing." His voice was steady, and he had willed himself to speak without breaking.

"We haven't seen him since he dropped you off at Nita's yesterday afternoon," he explained slowly. "We have been searching all night long without luck."

Pee-Paw was not one to sugarcoat, but his delivery was delicate and hopeful. Even at my age, I could tell that he truthfully didn't know what might happen. He knew not to promise that it would be all right, because it might not be.

His blue eyes were suddenly pools of water. He blinked quickly several times to release the buildup of tears and then quickly wiped his face.

There were no more words for what seemed like hours but must have been only a few minutes. The world lost all color to me. There was a bleakness introduced in those minutes, on that day, that has stayed with me. There was no Churchill joke to be made. There was no laughter or animated story or even prayer at that very moment. There was this silence that was filled with the loudest noise of tortured voices in our minds. It was the sharpest quiet I have ever known.

Mama broke down then. Now, it was clear to me why she looked the way she did this morning. Her cries were those of a tortured mother missing her child. The tears were real. The woman that had been consumed with what others thought about her couldn't care less. There was only one concern and it was the welfare of her child.

It's so simple to summarize but incredibly complex to grasp until you must.

Daddy quickly tried to wipe his tears as he just reached over to hug me. I hugged my daddy back as hard as I could. Gammy hugged both of us. Pee-Paw joined, followed by Mama in a ball sort of embrace that our family shared. If only for those brief minutes, it somehow made us feel whole. Still, the dimness was clear to all of us. We had lost our center, our Jackson. The connection he kept among all of us with his welcoming smile and heart of gold was already missing in the air that day.

Finally, we broke apart.

Daddy gathered his deep, composed voice and asked me if I had any questions. It was odd that I usually never shut my mouth, and I think they were all taken aback by my silence. The fact was, so many questions and thoughts were racing through my brain that I couldn't gather them up to make a sentence. My head was scrambled like Sunday morning eggs.

I grabbed my daddy's tough, callused hand. It was my turn to reciprocate for his years of defensiveness on my behalf. I knew he felt defeated for breaking. I wanted to make him feel empowered.

He felt foolish for brushing off Jackson's absence for so many hours that evening. I hoped Mama wouldn't bring it up again to make the cut any deeper. He needed to know that we still saw him for the strong person he had always been to us.

"Daddy, I love you and we will find him," I said, putting my head on his chest while simultaneously reaching for Mama.

"Oh, honey," Mama cried.

"We have been looking all night," she said, blowing her nose again.

"If Jackson had any control over the situation," she cried, "he would have gone to see Taft."

Then Mama continued, "He would never, ever put us all through this, and we all know that," Mama whispered while wiping tears from her swollen eyes.

"He was so excited about seeing Taft," she said, obviously fighting the emotion she simply could not control.

"Jackson! My Jackson is gone forever!"

Daddy had leaned over Mama and told her that she didn't know that.

Gammy had done her crying, which was apparent by her face the more I looked on. She must have done it privately. She never liked to show weakness, just love or the fight for love. She had all she could stand of the breakdown time for us. I was close enough to her to feel her spirit rehabilitating itself for a fight for Jackson. She was like a motor recharging. She was getting ready to speed race.

She walked over to the phone and began dialing those numbers. You know it wasn't push-button, just dial.

We could hear every dial return as her finger released the hole of the number. I heard her softly speaking to this one and that. She was collecting our immediate family to order. I knew it. Once she placed calls to the major hubs, which were the marina, church, and police stations, they would all communicate via CB, just as if they were hunting in the woods.

Sure as I had thought it, I started hearing trucks and cars pull into the drive.

First to arrive was Uncle Skeeter. He was one of the most loyal of the family. If you were his blood, he was protecting you.

Next was Uncle Taft, who was visibly shaken to the core over Jackson's disappearance.

Then my poor Aunt Sadie arrived. She was beaten down pretty bad by her sorry old husband Floyd. Pure D trash is what Floyd was, but when there was Churchill drama, he was sure to come around.

Then my Uncle Warren and his wife, Virginia, walked in.

As they entered each one kissed me then hugged Mama and Daddy, holding their heads down to show respect.

Gammy offered everyone coffee and ordered the church ladies in the kitchen. She told them we needed privacy to conduct what she called family business.

"Now Churchills," Gammy began, "what we have here is a situation that needs all of our blood kin working hard so we can fix it. One of our own is missing, and it's our job to find him."

Floyd, trash that he was, made a grumble sound under his breath. Even in the chaos of the situation, none of us will ever forget Gammy walking up behind his head and whacking him with her bare hand. The blow made him spit his Coca-Cola out in the air. He wiped it quickly with his bare arm.

"Dog, woman!" he yelled.

At this, the other men in the room stood glaring at him.

Gammy cleared her throat and went on to say there must be something we were not thinking about.

"Have any of you heard anything that we haven't discussed among other Churchills?" She asked. "Don't keep secrets," she ordered and stared at each of us.

It was then that I raised my hand.

"Don't raise your hand, granddaughter," Gammy said. "What is it?"

"Gammy?" My voice was quivering uncontrollably. "Tell me about the *searching* last night. I know Mr. Ledbetter was out until four in the morning and, when he got home, he was covered in mud. Where had he been and where are people thinking Jackson is? Not in the water!" I screamed and fell into tears again.

"No, no, not at all, baby girl," Daddy said as he put his arm around me.

He looked up at Gammy, "Huh, I didn't realize old Ledbetter was out helping last night."

Mama sniffled and explained that he told her that when she picked me up earlier.

"The Lord works in mysterious ways, I do declare," Gammy said, closing her eyes, tilting her head up to heaven.

"Alfred Ledbetter never seems interested in any of us, but in crisis he must truly be a good man," she went on.

My mind raced, thinking about how quickly Gammy would have changed her way of thinking if she knew how he had treated me the night before. Why, he would be in about the same shape as poor old Floyd with a whacked head.

The awful experience with that man suddenly seemed so unimportant. Now, none of it mattered.

For some reason, at this point, my head started spinning. I couldn't take in the information.

Where was Jackson? The one I ran to when I was afraid. Where was he? Maybe it was just some trick, but Mama was right. He would never hurt us that way.

Suddenly I was running outside. I remember hearing Gammy call out to me, but I couldn't seem to stop running. I heard the screen door pop behind me and knew she sent someone out to watch over me.

It was my Uncle Skeeter. He had followed me until I sat down in front of the water. It was low tide. He sat right down in the sand with me. We said nothing for a while.

Finally, Uncle Skeeter broke the silence and said simply, "Caroline, we are going to be OK, darlin."

We stared at the water awhile longer, filling the space without words. The water was a comfort to all of us, and for that reason, I somehow knew it hadn't taken Jackson away, on purpose or by accident.

"I want him back, Uncle Skeeter!" I hollered. "I want Jackson to walk right up here and tell us it was a big fat joke!" I cried.

Uncle Skeeter reached over and hugged me. He rocked me, holding me tightly, daring the world to hurt me.

Then Skeeter said, "I can see him now, making fun of us for our production over this so-called crisis. He will shrug his shoulders in that Jackson way. Then he'll tell us that he was fishin' and his motor choked out," he said as he mimicked Jackson's voice.

Skeeter and I broke into laughter. We would continue and then slow it down before giggling again and again. This was not because it was that funny. We just needed the release to carry us up to a better place than we had been.

Skeeter walked me back to my house because he thought I needed to be alone some. It would have normally been a peaceful evening walk down the coast and up the trail. On that day; however, the silence was broken with the calling out to our Jackson in the marshes.

Chapter 14

SECRETS REVEALED
1978

As Uncle Skeeter and I approached my house, leaving the other family at gammy and Pee-paws, I noticed flowers on the front porch steps. They were gardenias in a glass vase with pink ribbon beautifully tied around the top. The flowers were from Nita and Mrs. Ledbetter. Nita had put heart stickers on the vase for me. The card said: *Best Friends, Nita.*

I walked into our house feeling as if time had stopped. Jackson's camp T-shirt was hanging to dry outside the laundry room. Our baby portraits were hanging in the foyer just the same as they had been since I could remember.

I ran upstairs as Uncle Skeeter just sat down on the couch with his head buried in his hands.

"If you need me, I'm here, Caroline," he yelled up to me.

I ran into Jackson's room, falling onto his bed. I cried as I never had before. Tears of fear and rage were streaming uncontrollably from my eyes. The room smelled like him and felt like he was there. I grabbed his blanket and pressed it tightly to my nose. I breathed my brother's smell as deeply as I could into my lungs. The tears felt good to me. They felt real in a way that words couldn't have. Our family was too tender to talk to about any of it. Crying felt right and good to me. So, I did just that for the longest time. Finally, I stopped and my body felt exhausted even though I hadn't moved. Now that I have been in therapy, I know this is called emotional stress.

Then I remembered the letter from the morning I took it out of the dresser. I ran into my room and read it.

After about an hour, Skeeter called up to me, "You all right, Caroline?"

I honked my nose real loud and shouted, "*Yes*, I'm fine, Uncle Skeeter.

"Can you get Uncle Taft to come over here for a while?"

"Yes, ma'am!" he said. I could hear him getting Taft on the phone.

Once Taft arrived, I shared the letter with him: the apology from my missing brother to my uncle who I knew loved him.

He looked like he couldn't breathe after reading it. He got up and walked around the room, and then sat back down on the bed again.

"Caroline, I'm all screwed up!"

"No you're not. Why would you say that?"

"I just don't know who I am or where I fit in."

"You fit in right here with the Churchills."

"No, I don't! I never have!" Taft yelled as he started crying like a child.

"Jackson was the only person who never really judged me. Once he beat the tar out of the Walker boys for calling me a fag because I walked funny."

"Well, The Walker boys were always full of it. Jackson just knew they were being mean. There's nothing wrong with the way you walk."

Then I stood up and mimicked his walk which we all knew was a little funny.

Taft started laughing through his tears. He grabbed me and then the laughter turned into whelping cries. He was shaking and squeezing me as he cried. I just rubbed his back realizing he needed me. Even then at my young age I somehow knew that his conflict was far deeper than I could comprehend. I didn't want to know more.

Uncle Skeeter heard the commotion and yelled, "Ya'll alright up there?"

"Yes, Uncle Skeeter," I said with a straight voice.

Finally Taft composed himself and gently grabbed my head to look straight into my eyes.

"Caroline, I don't know what to say."

"Just say it," I demanded.

"Jackson and I had our first real disagreement the other day."

Taft paused struggling to find the right words to say.

"I'm different Caroline. Jackson knew it and he was tryin' to help me."

I didn't want to hear much more. Uncle Taft was about to out himself because he was caught in this broken moment. Later, he would regret it and he and I would have awkwardness between us.

He wiped his face with Jackson's bed sheet and started, "There was a real nice group of guys at school. One in particular wanted me to start up a band with him. He was an odd guy and I wasn't sure if he thought I was..." he stopped.

"Gay?" The word had left my mouth before getting permission from my brain. For some reason, it needed to be said and if I had thought more about it I would have neglected the urge.

My Uncle could have hit me or cried or...

Instead, he reached over and hugged me so hard I had to pull away to catch my breath.

Even in that magnificent second of honesty, the inference was never confirmed. The fact that I said it and he left it to fly in the air without denial conveyed what needed to be said between us.

In our Churchill forward march Taft continued.

"Jackson wanted me to quit the band and get away from the guy. I liked being a part of the group and I wasn't sure how I really felt about..."

I sat still just rubbing his back as he spoke taking frequent breaks to collect himself.

"We argued, and I said some mean things to Jackson."

I tried to reassure him. "You know Jackson probably understood. He was excited about seeing you at the fish fry."

"The truth of it is that Jackson really talked some sense into me. It wasn't about my life choices but the fact that this guy was so weird. He wanted to control me in every way. It went to the point that I was getting scared. Jackson told me he didn't care who I was as long as I was safe."

"Don't you see Caroline? I may never be able to apologize to him now!" He said breaking into tears again.

Finally he asked, "Would you mind not mentioning this to the rest of the family? This was Jackson's and my personal business, and we were handling it on our own," he said as he put his arm around me.

"Your secret is good with me, Uncle Taft. I know Jackson usually agrees with you and he probably would about this too," I said, giving him a hug.

Chapter 15

MAMA'S RULES
1978

The next morning, I walked into the kitchen and saw my poor daddy staring into the morning newspaper. The city headline was about Jackson. It was suspected that there was a sexual pervert running the roads of our beaches. Citizens were encouraged to lock their doors at all times and never leave their children unattended. "Please walk in pairs and never alone until this person is apprehended." There was nothing to prove any of it at the time but the rumor mill had officially started.

I was trying to be useful that morning 'cause Gammy said we all had to do our part for Jackson. I answered the phone for a few hours, taking my job very seriously. I logged in each call on a clipboard Uncle Warren put together, with the person's name and return number. The detectives had suggested this just in case it helped them figure out where they might look for my brother.

Search parties continued, and our church had prayer twice a day. It was evident that Jackson had made it to the Baileys' and done his chores there.

The Baileys' property was the most densely wooded on the island, which made it a major search target. It was covered in thick marsh, backed up to pine and palm trees. It was difficult to walk through because the water used to rise up just high enough that you could bog right down and get your feet stuck. This was one of Jackson and Taft's favorite fishing spots. They had played there for many years with the Bailey boys.

At 3:10 in the afternoon, a policeman assistant by the name of Simon Osbourne called and asked for Mama. I told him she was gone, and he asked if I knew the young man who was missing. Once I explained that he was my brother, he asked me if Jackson had a dentist. I thought that was the strangest question. Then he asked if Daddy was there. I walked into the kitchen where Daddy was standing dazed and handed him the phone before walking onto the back porch.

Once outside I saw that the cable news had come to Culley. They interviewed everyone and even did footage of the men searching. The city folks seemed to be entertained by watching our airboats chug through the marshes yelling my brother's name.

It was the first time I heard Jackson referred to as a body. The news lady was looking into the camera, when her words sent a chill down my spine, "So far, there are only rumors without confirmation of a body being recovered."

Pastor Caldwell's wife, Toot, grabbed me and walked me inside the minute she heard it. Moments later, Gammy rocked me on her porch, singing "Jesus Loves Me" in country time.

Uncle Taft had approached us on the porch, knelt down beside the rocker, and started crying. It seemed that there was an intrinsic reality that had taken us over. We didn't know anything for sure but we had enough common sense to realize that the end result couldn't be a good one. The severity of the unspoken fear haunted us all during the days of the search for Jackson. It was one that I had never experienced in our light hearted family.

Gammy looked up at Pee-Paw as her rocking chair bumped across the wood. "Our Churchills are fallin' apart, Buckley."

He grabbed her hand and squeezed it, staring off in disbelief. I sat on my grandma's lap, really too big to do so but so glad she still let me.

Then a dark car followed by quiet police cars pulled into the dirt drive. Gammy looked up at Pee-Paw, who yelled out for my daddy. Mama walked out and started screaming *no* over and over. The church ladies guarded her like she was a diamond, trying to shield her from the reality that was most likely coming our way.

Two large men dressed in suits walked up the porch steps. The hard soles of their shoes made deep thumping sounds on the wood. The officers quietly got out of their cars. They stood outside of their vehicles with their hats over the hearts and heads down. Gammy scanned their faces and when they wouldn't return eye contact with her she seemed to understand the purpose of their visit. Most of those officers had grown up fishing and worshipping around gammy and Pee-paw. They were there to show respect and support.

One of the men asked to speak to Mama and Daddy privately. Gammy stood pushing me aside from the rocker. She clinched her hands into fists and began clearing the way to her parlor. No one spoke a word. The church ladies formed a circle and held hands as they released mama to join the men and daddy in the parlor. It was a quiet room never used but always elegant. Gammy held the door open and closed it behind them. Neither before that day nor since did I ever see my gammy have absolutely no expression on her face. She was blank. The blankness spoke volumes to me that day.

It wasn't even a solid minute after the parlor doors closed when we heard the first of my mama's primal screams. All of the aunts and uncles and church folks knew that the hopefulness that we desired had come to an end.

A body had been found on Double Barrel and Thyra Bailey's property. The officers knew that it was Jackson because they had known him since birth. Daddy still insisted that a family member identify the body. Although Daddy wanted to go, neither Gammy nor Mama would allow it.

Uncle Skeeter, Uncle Taft, and Uncle Warren went together to the coroner's office. Two of my uncles returned in grim silence. Taft had gotten sick in the yard and couldn't even come inside.

Uncle Skeeter announced grimly, "Our Jackson is gone."

After Uncle Skeeter confirmed what we had known for two days, we all embraced one another quietly.

"Our Jackson is with Jesus," Gammy screamed. "Jackson is home with the Lord!" she chanted with her eyes shut tightly just before she started wailing with tears.

Shortly after that, Gammy took her phone off the hook so it would stop ringing. Word had gotten out that Double Barrel had gone crazy about someone hurting Jackson on his property. He had his guns out and was gathering men for an old fashioned man hunt. Many of the locals had an interest in helping old Double Barrel and were starting to call. Gammy batted the church ladies back into the kitchen as they walked in to offer coffee.

We could hear her talking with Toot Caldwell.

"Toot, now we love ya'll and are happy to have the help, but we are in need of some privacy. Whenever this here door is shut," Gammy said, pointing to the obvious door as if there may have been confusion, "we want to be left alone except for your husband so he can bless us, OK, darlin'?"

"I've got it, Mavis," Toot replied like an officer.

Toot had round-the-clock signups for Gammy and Mama's kitchens. Neither of them were to wash a dish or prepare a meal until they could get their nerves together.

Gammy started yelling out Bible verses rather than cussin'. I knew this had been one of her methods of dealing with the urge to cuss for many years. Sometimes it worked and sometimes it didn't.

She yelled in a controlled voice, "*Revelation 21:8*. But as for the cowardly, the faithless, the detestable, as for murderers, the sexually immoral, sorcerers, idolaters, and all liars, their portion will be in the lake that burns with fire and sulfur, which is the second death."

Gammy continued, "James so whoever knows the right thing to do and fails to do it, for him it is sin."

Under her breath, she couldn't control herself.

"The nerve of that damned evil ass comin' up here on Churchill property and hurtin' one of my own." She screamed, "I will cut off his balls myself and serve 'em to the baitfish!"

Gammy's words proved she had lost control.

"Lord help me! That SOB will be found and punished if I do it my own damn self," she continued yelling.

Pee-Paw now stood and walked over to Gammy to help control her.

"Sit down, dear," he said. "You can't go on spittin' ugly language to your young'ins and grandbabies," he whispered in his polite voice.

"I know that, Buckley Churchill, because some evil-assed sinner has been allowed to come on our land and kill one of my grandbabies, *my Jackson!*" she screamed, hitting the wall.

We noticed Floyd moving away, realizing she might use him as an unfortunate target during her tirade.

At this, Mama Shug just fell onto the floor. She wasn't conscious. The church ladies ran in the minute Mama hit the floor, which confirmed they were listening to every word from the kitchen.

The ladies were standing over Mama, fanning her with their hands.

Toot started praying, and Gammy joined her. Finally, they were all praying in unison as if they were at Sunday service.

Gammy was on fire and couldn't stop.

"He will pay!" Gammy shouted.

Uncle Skeeter and Uncle Warren now stood ready to contribute.

"Whatcha want us to do, Mama?" they asked, ready to go.

Gammy started telling about Double Barrel and his hunting group when paster Caldwell started humming. Then he stood in the back of the room and started chanting, "Be gone, devil! You back away from our holiness!"

Pee-Paw and I were darting our eyes back and forth from the ladies to Pastor Caldwell to Mama. We couldn't move.

Suzie Ledbetter ran in about then and held out a towel with some rubbing alcohol on it. She stuck it right by Mama's nose for her to breathe. Just then, Mama's eyes popped open and she started coughing as she looked around, remembering the hellish situation with which we were dealing.

"*Praise God!*" all of the women said in song.

Then they went back into the kitchen as if it had never happened. The ice was steadily going into the glasses, and the pies were being pulled out of the oven. As guests visited to check on the family, they were not permitted to see us per Gammy's request. They were fed and given cold sweet tea.

It was all so dramatic, yet we were all just sitting and staring like we were sedated. We heard all of the noises of normalcy going on in the kitchen and the yard. I am now told it's called shock. Gammy is the only one who didn't succumb to it.

"*I want justice, dammit!*" Gammy said, still defying the quiet of the room.

Pastor Caldwell chanted with his eyes shut tightly, "Let it out, Sister Mavis Churchill. God forgive her for the language, but let her reach out and share herself with us all who love her." He continued, "Sister Mavis Churchill, you tell that devil that you will fight him in the name of Jesus Christ our Lord."

"AMEN!" Pee-Paw shouted, followed by each of his sons.

Mama slowly stood up and raised her voice at everyone in the room for the first time in all of her years as a Churchill.

"You all listen to me and you listen well," she said as she blew the hair out of her face. Black mascara was running down her cheeks and her clothes were wrinkled.

She couldn't care less about her appearance, or if her words hurt anyone around her. Gammy sat still in surprise.

"My baby is gone," she said in a low voice. "I have known it since Saturday afternoon. Mothers always know. *Always!*" Mama ranted.

"No one can bring him back," she continued. "Do you think for one damn minute I want to hear any of the details of how this happened? Do any of you want to know what was done to my boy? *Do you?*" she shouted in a whimpering yet loud voice.

"The last thing in the world I want is for Double Barrel Bailey, God love him, gettin' liquored up and shootin' up the town. We would be all over the news and everybody would be talking about our Jackson!"

"If we make a scene out of it, everybody will start running their mouths. We will go to court and have to sit there and listen to it," she explained. "Maybe they will even show us pictures. *No, no, no!* I simply won't allow it. Do you all hear me?" Mama stood there for a moment.

"We are going to get through these next few days and give my boy a proper funeral service," she said, trying to compose herself. "We are going to be proper about it in honor of Jackson. There will be no more cussing, yellin', or gossiping, going on about any of these details.

"Jackson died on a rock by the Baileys' house," Mama said in a trancelike stare. "You know that big one that he and Taft used to fish from for years. He fell asleep right there. It was peaceful. He just fell asleep," she said, dazed.

Daddy looked at her, confused by what she was saying.

She walked over to Sadie's white trash husband, Floyd. Gammy followed her eyes to Floyd and squinted as if she could shoot him.

Then Mama said the meanest thing I have ever heard her say in her life.

"Floyd, if I hear that you have discussed any of Jackson's personal business, I will take out your eyeballs with my Sunday meat fork," Mama said, staring at him.

"If you do not believe me, sir, you just try me," she went on. "I am just mad enough right now that I may do it anyway."

"Shug, I would never..."

"SHUT UP!" Mama yelled. "You good-for-nothin' piece of trash!

"You never gave Jackson the time of day!" she screamed. "You wouldn't be here now if it weren't for you being so dang nosy, and we all know it! If this would have been anything that didn't interest your warped mind, you would have just sat in your blue recliner drinking beer all day."

Gammy's eyes opened wider than I knew they could just before she cheered, "*Amen!*"

Then under Gammy's breath, she started her nasty talk again.

Mama interrupted Gammy and continued in a calmer voice, "We are going to let this end now. I will not allow anyone to discuss what happened to Jackson or how he was found. Do you all understand me?" she asked, looking around the room.

"Gammy, that includes you too," Mama said, looking straight into Gammy's eyes.

I read Pee-Paw's lips as he said, "Jesus in heaven." He feared Gammy's response to Mama. This could have been all-out war with the emotions running as high as they were. We all knew it. The room went silent, as did the kitchen.

"Whatever you say, Sugar," Gammy said so softly.

Everyone seemed to exhale with relief. The church ladies started back up loud conversation in the kitchen as well.

All heads were shaking in agreement.

So there it was. We were given rules for how we would grieve for Jackson: the murder we couldn't discuss because Mama said so. We were to pretend he fell asleep on a rock that he used to fish on. It sat in our minds like a parked car. No exploration allowed. Do not enter.

Chapter 16

OPENED DOORS, UNWANTED ATTENTION
2001

Dr. Chapman's office sometimes smelled of peppermint tobacco, if there is such a thing. I kind of liked it, except that the smell told my brain that I was about to be upset because I was in the *doctor's office.*

I waited patiently trying to find comfort in the classical music as I watched the busy receptionist.

As I reached for my cup of coffee, I noticed that today's mug read: "Words, like nature, half reveal and half conceal the soul within."

"Caroline, what do you think about your life since your brother died?" Doc asked while sipping his hot tea.

I lay back on the sofa and closed my eyes, focusing on a perfect mind picture of Jackson smiling back at me, gesturing me to go on.

Slowly, I searched my mind for words that made sense.

"After Jackson was gone, everything became dismal. I didn't know who to talk to about any of it. We all just pretended that we were fine. Jackson's bedroom door was locked up. The whereabouts of the key were never disclosed. We couldn't discuss it. Our lives had become a make-believe game. Gammy used to try to give me opportunities to talk about it, but I was scared I would get her in trouble with Mama. I used to feel so guilty for not sharin' everything with her. I regret that today.

"Now, so much time has passed it would be foolish to talk with her about it." I looked down at my feet, unable to process my thoughts now.

"Doc, truthfully, I can't even remember the entire service we had for my brother. I recall certain parts of the day. There was an enormous picture of Jackson displayed beside the casket. He was in his church suit with a big smile on his face. The casket was closed, so we couldn't see him. I was never sure he was even in it, which I realize is a child's silly imagination.

"Pastor Caldwell started with the scripture *John 14:27*," I said almost in a trance.

"Forgive me, Caroline, but I don't know scriptures by heart. Do you know that particular one?"

I started chanting it like a preacher.

"I am leaving you with a gift—peace of mind and heart. And the peace I give is a gift the world cannot give. So don't be troubled or afraid," I said as if making a speech at a podium.

Doc Chapman clapped his hands to humor me about my knowledge of scripture.

"Then Pastor went right into telling everyone there about Jackson and me that morning. I remember that people brought so much food, we had to throw some of it out."

We sat in the silence for another second. I had to force the memories.

"Even Mr. and Mrs. Ledbetter came over with several dishes of food. This wouldn't have been weird if she had brought it alone." I paused.

"How do you feel about Alfred Ledbetter?" Doc asked. "You told me he was unkind to you at the sleepover that night.

"Well, actually on one of their bereavement visits, he took me out into the backyard and apologized for being so mean at the party. He told me that his brother went missing when he was a teenager and the entire evening had brought back some troubling memories for him. He explained that this is why he began researching medications for underprivileged children. His brother had epilepsy and had an attack too far from home one afternoon. It had taken them days to locate his body. Now, his reactions that night seemed a little easier for me to stomach. He even started attending church after Jackson's death. Gammy says it made him take stock of how lucky he was. He's been baptized now," I said, looking over at Doc Chapman as if this had fixed everything.

"His daughter Nita and I are still the best of friends. She seems happy but doesn't want serious relationships," I said, realizing I was getting off track.

"Let's not lose focus, Caroline," Doc redirected me.

"Did you and Nita ever discuss how her father treated you at her party that evening?"

"Just a little. That would crush her."

"Is she that fragile?"

I thought for a bit before answering.

"Nita has never really talked about her daddy with me, except when we were young she used to remind me to be extra quiet when he was home. It seems to be a taboo subject. She loves him and I don't think he has ever hurt her but she knows he doesn't fit in. I believe she and her mama try to keep him out of any of the town gossip."

"I see." Doc said while considering my answer.

"I remember after talking to Mr. Ledbetter, I had gone upstairs and just sat in Jackson's room. This was days before it became an off-limits area in the house. I looked in his closet and went through all of his pockets, searching for any part of him I could find. I wanted a new secret or story from my brother, and since he couldn't talk to me I thought I would search for one."

I stopped and took a drink of water while Dr. Chapman looked on.

"He had this fishing jacket with pockets all over it. Jackson loved that old thing," I said, smiling.

"I found a key inside of it. I kept it along with some photos and stones that he had once told me would bring me calm. You know, I still have those things in my secret box? There isn't a week that goes by that I don't pull them out and just touch them."

"I see. Is that your secret deposit box by the sea?" he asked.

"Yes, of course," I said shyly.

"It has so many private things in it, just like Jackson told me it would," I continued.

"Do you have it hidden well?" Doc asked.

"Yes, and only my Wit knows where it is," I told him proudly.

"Daddy made one for Wit too. He hides his all over the place. He still changes his locations like Jackson taught me to do. I don't change my locations because I couldn't risk the box getting dirty or worn down. Jackson couldn't build me another one," I said, looking away.

"I guess it's somewhat of a tradition that Jackson has passed down now that Wit has one, huh?" I said.

"Any idea what the key you found may go to, Caroline?" he probed.

I laughed, thinking of Jackson. "Oh, there is no telling," I said. "The one thing I am certain of it's somewhere he probably didn't need to be. I figure an old door that probably doesn't exist anymore or it could just be something he found one day in the ocean."

"In your heart, who do you think hurt your brother?" he asked.

Reflective, I said, "Well, there were times I wondered about Mr. Ledbetter, since he is so cuss mean.

"I told Pastor and Daddy about him being kind of mean to me. I never explained all of it to Daddy. After that, he talked to the Marine Patrol and asked if Mr. Ledbetter helped in the search. It was confirmed that he helped for a long time that night. He was dismissed as a consideration."

I continued, "Then there was Ustus. He was so beaten down and pitiful he wouldn't have ever hurt a fly. Daddy mentioned him to me, and I felt certain we could rule him out.

"For years the detectives would come down and ask questions, because in the city there was another similar case," I explained.

"They thought they may have a serial killer on their hands."

"What do you believe, Caroline?" Doc Chapman asked, leaning over in his chair, showing eagerness.

"Doc, I will tell you that anyone who could possibly hurt Jackson was pure evil," I said. "In my mind, I picture a monster. Whoever hurt him had to be someone not even human in nature. Something visiting that we just didn't notice, maybe. The idea of wanting anything less than friendship from Jackson seemed inconceivable to me."

I started crying again.

"Do you feel that your entire family wants to move forward?" he asked, staring into my eyes.

"All except Mama," I said. "They want to move on but they can't. I can't. It changed us, but we don't want to admit it. We all have empty spots now even in our conversations. We will start to talk about it and feel an immediate slap of silence because Mama said we couldn't. It seemed as wrong as stealin' to talk about it among our family.

"Mama has made her position on the subject clear. We seem to go from the morning being so nice to him missing. We never go into detail about the way we found him," I said behind tears.

"You have said this makes you angry," he said, "but have you thought more about how you may take control of that anger?"

"I need to stop feeling so weak and powerless," I said. "My jumps from the dock help," I explained, smiling.

"I feel like I have betrayed Jackson somehow by not getting to the bottom of it all. He had that terrible experience at the end, so I should be able to think about it with him," I said.

"Do you *need* to know what happened?" he continued.

"It doesn't matter what I need," I said.

"Yes, it does!" Doc yelled. "Fight for yourself, Caroline!"

"We can't figure it out if special agents couldn't. That's what Daddy has always said."

I could feel the weakness filling up in my throat again.

I needed to say it out loud. I needed to hear myself say what hurt me so much and I never could talk about. That is what this damn therapy was about. *I will say it*, I thought.

I could feel Jackson telling me to go on. It was OK.

"They found him in between Mr. and Mrs. Bailey's property line and my house," I said as I sniffed, catching my breath. "We couldn't even have an open casket because he was so messed up," I continued, now feeling my face heat up.

Doc handed me a wad of tissues.

"I know this is difficult for you, Caroline," he said.

"My beautiful Jackson wasn't even presentable." I pouted angrily.

As I said this to the doctor, my mind started racing. This is what had to be done. It was there that I made that decision. *So this is what therapy is all about.*

I could barely hear Doc talking now. I was in my own world. I pleasantly left without disclosing my plans.

I could hardly wait to go to the courthouse over in the city and start my own investigation about Jackson. Never once before had I ever contemplated doing this without the support of my family. Something struck me on that day and I had to find out more.

I used my cell phone to make a few calls to the city. It took me minutes to find out that Detective Osbourne was the assisting policeman who was working with the detectives on the case in the 70's. He mainly worked in cold cases now which made him the perfect person for me to see.

His secretary told me that he could see me right then if I could swing by the courthouse. She explained that once she told him who I was he was more than happy to accommodate me.

Doc may just be right, I thought. *I can investigate on my own to bring closure for myself.*

As I pulled into the parking lot at the courthouse, my stomach was in knots. My mama would have my head if she had any idea that I was going to start my own investigation.

* * *

He was positioned in a cubicle with full view of Detective Osbourne's office. He looked on as Osbourne recognized Caroline immediately. He focused with intensity on the movement of their lips and hand gestures. No one even noticed him. After all, he worked in the courthouse and mimicked normal behaviors fraught with superficial charm.

He noticed how they warmly greeted one another. Osbourne's bleeding heart would likely force him back into fixation with the case again, he thought.

"*So Caroline, you dare to challenge me after all of these years?*" he said to himself in a high-pitched voice, wiping sweat that poured from his head.

"*I outwitted my brilliant father. You will be no contest,*" he thought to himself.

"*Game on!*" he whispered while drilling a toothpick between his side teeth.

Chapter 17

THE ROCK AT THE BAILEY'S
2001

Old Double Barrel Bailey had become bored once all of his boys stopped playin' college football. He still managed to keep about eight good hunting dogs caged up on his property. Lord, help me as his full-time neighbor.

They sold the old Winnebago, and he continuously drove us all crazy with his projects. This month, he started a tree-clearing project for the first time since he had lived in the house. His loud machines gave game to Mama's horn honking outside in the mornings. All of that noise combined with the fact that I couldn't get Wit to come downstairs for the life of me was making my nerves crazy.

I banged on his door, feeling as if the entire house was shaking. "Son, don't you make me break this door down!" I threatened.

My nerves were shot with every honk of Mama's horn, followed by Double Barrel yelling, "*Timberrrr.*" I was just about to start kicking the door when he gingerly opened it, shooting me those bright straight teeth and saluting me like a military officer.

"I'm ready, Mama," he said as if I hadn't been begging him to come out for fifteen minutes.

"What in God's creation were you doing in there that you couldn't come out when I called you?" I demanded.

"Uh, well, you know that Mr. Bailey is clearing all of those trees in between our property and theirs, right?" he said.

"Wit, of course I know that," I shouted over the wood chipper audible inside our home.

"Well, I've been finding all kinds of prizes over there," Wit explained. "Some fit in my secret box and some don't, but it's my imagination time with them, Mama."

As I shooed him out of his room and down the stairs, I had to ask. "What kinds of things have you managed to find over there, son?"

"Oh, a hand knife and wood and..." His words were halted by another one of Mama's car horn honks, which were coming more quickly now.

"OK, have a good day," I said, giving him his lunch-box and waving out to a now impatient Mama.

I watched them leaving the drive; I could see Mama's bouffant moving side to side. Then I remembered the condition of Wit's room upstairs. He hadn't even considered making his bed, and there were toys all over the floor.

I darted back up there and started putting them away. As I was pulling the quilt back, my toe hit something underneath.

I got down on my knees and pulled out an old piece of driftwood.

It seemed familiar to me but I couldn't remember why. It was almost in the shape of the state of Florida. I studied it for a while and even took it downstairs to think about it while I had my coffee.

As I was flipping through the newspaper, I heard Pee-Paw outside, whistling as he often did to alert us to his presence.

Suddenly, Tripod started yelping, and I saw Pee-Paw's sweet face looking through the screen door.

"Dear, you decent?" he asked, halfway smiling.

"Yeah Pee-Paw," I said, "I have my drawers on," I teased back.

The screen opened and it popped shut behind him. He had a sandwich bag of trout fillets in his hand.

"Gammy has directed me to bring these over for you. Pastor's wife brought us a mess of fish last night that we can't begin to eat on our own."

"Oh, thank you, Pee-Paw," I said, grabbing the fish and putting them in the refrigerator.

"Want a cup of coffee?" I asked while already pouring it, adding the proper amounts of cream and sugar.

"Thank ya, dear," he said, reaching for the coffee as he noticed the driftwood on the table.

"Where in the world did you find this, granddaughter?" he asked with positive curiosity.

I explained that Wit had been snooping around Double Barrel's property where the trees were coming down. Pee-Paw and I exchanged a look with no words.

Pee-Paw broke the silence. "I swear it sure looks like the piece of wood that Taft and Jackson found when they were scalloping one summer. They argued over who found it, and I tried to calm them down talking about the shape of it. Sure looks like our state to me.

"What was that picture ya'll all went to see in the city so many times?" Pee-Paw asked. "That one with the aliens and that dark man who thought he had asthma? He took them deep breaths," Pee-Paw asked softly, kind of grinning.

"*Star Wars*?" I asked, laughing out loud.

"I guess so," he said, grinning. "Anyhow, the boys used to pretend that it was one of them lighted-up wands," he went on.

"Light sabers," I corrected, and he smiled back at me.

"Why, they would fight over who got this driftwood and who got a plain old stick. Of course, this may not be it but it sure looks similar, don't it?" he said, looking over the piece with careful observation.

For some reason, Darth Vader and driftwood fights were not jogging my memory. After Pee-Paw left, I went to my credenza and pulled out the papers I had gotten from the city police station the day before.

I grabbed a cup of coffee along with the papers, and out to the dock I went.

Tripod was following me with his sideways walk. Once I got there, I did what I always did, which was get my key attached by Velcro behind my bench seat. I unlocked the storage area under the bench.. People assumed I kept books and Coca-Colas in it. They were, in fact, correct, but I also had something else sacred in it. I plunked down and tenderly pulled out my safety deposit box by the sea.

It was still as beautiful as the day Jackson gave it to me. I had small folded pieces of paper in there from just days after he left us. It carried me through times of high school love triangles, college, marriage, and childbirth.

Then, of course, there were the things I had once found in Jackson's jacket after he left us. I often talked to it, although I don't like admitting that to people 'cause they might think I'm half crazy.

Slowly, I started opening and rereading the copies of the newspaper clippings I had gotten from Detective Osbourne the day before.

Ted Marshall, 24 years of age, was reported missing August 10, 1983. His body was found in shallow water four days later near the boat ramp at Seaside Paradise. His parents have been notified and services will be held August 18 at the Seaside Presbyterian Fellowship Hall.

I'm not lying when I say that I could so strongly feel Jackson pulling me along. I was feeling stronger about facing things than I ever had before.

Detective Osbourne had explained that the Marshall family still lived in Seaside City in the same home.

He promised that he would leave a message for the Marshalls and give them my number. He told me he couldn't give me theirs but he could do it the other way and see if they tried to reach me.

I read the article over and over and thought about the murders. The age of the other boy was different. The condition of the bodies was similar.

I glared off into the sun-reflecting water and whispered, "What happened to you, Jackson? What do you think I should know?"

At this, Tripod and I started exiting the dock. I was still in my sweats from sleep but it didn't matter to me. I could vaguely hear Mama's voice in my conscience, "Caroline, do you just want to turn into a hippie?"

I could feel my speed pick up in my step as I was walking toward the Baileys'. Mr. Bailey saw me coming and took his sun hat off to show me respect.

"Hey, Double Barrel!" I shouted as he motioned for his lumberjack to turn off the machinery.

"Are we bothering you, Caroline, with this loud mess?" Mr. Bailey asked.

"Oh, no, you know me better than that," I lied.

"I hope my little Wit isn't driving you crazy coming over here so often." I steadied myself with this trivia.

"Shoot, no!" he said. "I love having him come over and watch these machines. Wit loves it too. I raised my share of boys, ya know?"

"He has been exploring quite a bit," Double Barrel said. "That's what young'ins is supposed to do, ain't it?" he went on, holding onto his hat.

I couldn't help but stare at the empty spot where I had come for so many years. The place where a searcher noticed a red shirt and walked over to find my brother lying in the marsh, partially submerged in the salt water he loved so much. I could still hear the call of his name that went on for a few days.

My mind suddenly raced back to that day after my uncles returned; we walked over to the property line between what is now my home and the Baileys', and stared at this spot. Mama was given some strong nerve pills, and we didn't hear from her except for the day of the service.

She took a liking to the medicine and lay in bed for a few years, come to think of it. Gammy and the church ladies would come over and read scriptures to her, but other than that, she stayed put most of the time.

I had run over, with Daddy trying to hold me back, and seen some of the red still on the rock. My brother's blood no doubt. I had sat on the rock, right in the red. I touched the rock, wanting to be close to Jackson's last place. The policeman moved me, and I screamed as if he was taking Jackson away from me again. Yes, it was a scene, but I wouldn't change it. I wanted him back.

Pee-Paw was asking questions about the body. Skeeter whispered, "Nobody needs to ever know about it, Daddy."

Pee-Paw quietly looked out at the rock with his crystal blue eyes filling with tears. Taft seemed to stay nauseated after he saw Jackson at the coroner's office. Gammy says he lost thirty pounds that summer.

I snapped out of my dream state when Mrs. Bailey joined us and was raising her voice to get my attention. My mind jolted back into the present, and I realized she was asking me how my pee-paw and gammy were doing.

"Oh, fine, just fine!" I said.

"Pee-Paw was over this morning bringing me some fish," I continued.

I looked at the elderly couple for a minute as they leaned forward.

"May I walk around some and look?" I whispered. "You know?" I said, putting my head down.

"Yeah, girl," Double Barrel said nervously, "I told ya'll when that awful thang happened. You come over here to that spot any time you want to. You know that we won't touch that big ole' rock...Clearing these trees makes it look different from how it did when, uhh, mmmm..." He couldn't find the words.

"I know," I said to help him out, giving him a strong look in the eyes to show my appreciation.

I started walking over, and as I got closer, my body started shaking. This place was both good and bad for me.

It was the ending of a beautiful life and the last place that life existed.

It was a place where we played and fished as children. It was a place where for a long while our family would imagine the most awful things that one of our own had experienced at the hands of a crazy person.

I sat right there on that rock. The last place my brother had lived and the place he died. At least I was trying to learn about the day that Mama had hidden from us. I felt stronger for it.

Tripod was barking and digging near me, but I didn't think much of it. I yelled at him to hush so I could hear myself think.

He was a new addition to our family and was one of the most foolish cuss dogs we had ever owned.

Sand was sprinkling out behind him. He finally raised his head up and had a fiddler crab in his mouth. He strutted around on his three legs. He was showing it off, and then he would put it back down, before starting the chase all over again. He was an entertaining fool dog. Now, he stopped digging and proudly displayed a small box clutched in his teeth. He started trotting around the yard with his tail high in the air.

"Come here, you nutty dog!" I shouted. Tripod continued prancing with pride, holding his treasure pressed between his teeth. "If you found Wit's secret deposit box by the sea, he will kick your three-legged butt," I said, amusing myself.

Chapter 18

A New Baptist
2001

Culley Cove Baptist was buzzing Sunday morning. Mrs. Nellie Buckwelder's husband had come home from the city smelling like women's perfume. She was eighty-three years old, and Mr. Buckwelder could barely stand up straight. He likely hugged somebody at the doctor's appointment. Their own daughter had driven him to town, but poor ol' Nellie was starting to get loopy. Her daughter had put her on nerve pills, and Gammy suspected this was the reason her mind was slipping.

Ol' Mrs. Nellie had stood up during service and told about her husband and what her suspicions were. She then went so far as to notify all of the women in the congregation that if they wanted poor ol' Mr. Buckwelder, they could have him.

For a moment, the only sounds heard were the beeps from the old men's hearing aids as they adjusted them. The old-timers could tell that something was going on worth hearing and were trying to listen. This was a common sound in the church pews when something juicy was going on.

Pastor Caldwell cleared his throat and asked everyone to remain seated while one of the clergy escorted Nellie outside. I couldn't help but glance over at Gammy. Her perfectly teased head was steadily shaking as she kept her eyes closed. My mama was patting down her dress, which was her nervous tick.

Nita and I were seated beside one another near the middle of the church. She and I ran the Baptist Church Ladies Committee and were having a congregation feast after service that day.

Pastor asked us to stand as he reminded the congregation of our ladies luncheon following service. Suzie Ledbetter raised her hand like a school girl and added some gracious comments about some of our works. Her pride in Nita was evident as was her appreciation to me for our friendship. Alfred, who had started to attend Sunday service sat quietly beside her never looking up.

Pastor Caldwell went on to explain how hard we had worked to put these fine fixins' out on this lovely day. I couldn't help but watch Gammy as she gave eye bounces to each face, taking in their acknowledgement of her granddaughter doin' her part at the church house. It may sound somewhat corny but it has always made me proud to make my family feel good about my work.

Gammy's only daughter, Sadie, had married pure trash, as Gammy put it, and she would forever serve her sentence with that hateful cuss. He had limited poor Sadie's opportunities, Gammy said.

Cleeve and Wit were taking up the collection plates at the end of the pews. Wit paused and put his own three dollars in before starting to send the plate down the aisle. My mama was glowing with pride as she watched his love for his church. We are small town and we know it. There is an unspoken beauty in our actions, though, that I wouldn't trade for anything else in the world. This commitment to holding each other up can bring a family to glory or doom. There is a sense of pressure attached to pleasing so many others.

I suppose that through all of the commotion with Nellie Buckwelder and the luncheon credits that we didn't notice one of our new guests in the balcony. You have to understand that our old Culley Cove Baptist Church had become somewhat of a famous religious place in North Florida.

Pastor Caldwell and Toot had come in when they were in their early twenties and made a big difference in our congregation.

They had reached out to our neighboring beach communities and even a few of the cities. Some of our members would travel forty minutes or better to come in for Sunday and Wednesday services.

They would dine at our seafood restaurants before making their route back home. Visitors were always asked to stand, but there had begun to be so many of them that we no longer went around asking them to introduce themselves. Many of them were students driving in from the university.

After service, we walked out behind the church to the covered picnic area for the luncheon. It was our favorite gathering spot sitting on a beautiful lot right there on the beach. The children would often bring their swimsuits and play in the water afterwards. The adults would sit and talk for hours. The covered area provided a wonderful breeze for them to enjoy without overheating. It was expected that everyone would stay for the day and there was more than enough food for supper to be served before evening service. I was helping serve potato salad and deviled eggs when I noticed an interesting character among our church members. He had never been to our service before because the women would have certainly had an interest. He was movie star handsome with a tan punctuating the blue eyes like stars. His teeth were obviously bleached very white and his nails manicured to perfection. This man took care of himself yet I saw no wedding ring or tan line to suggest its removal.

I had Suzie Ledbetter take over serving for me so I could find out more about this stranger. I approached him and introduced myself.

"So you are Caroline Churchill Burton?" he asked, looking at me smugly.

"I'm sorry, do we know each other?" I bounced back.

The truth of the matter is he did look kind of familiar to me. I couldn't for the life of me remember from where though. You know when someone reminds you of something before but you can't place it. Your mind spins but never finds the connection.

That is exactly what happened to me that day right there in the back of the church house with this man.

At this, Cleeve made his way over, curious about the handsome visitor.

"I am Chandler Monnier," he said proudly, as if it should mean something to us.

Clearly gathering from our expressions that we were clueless to his importance, he added, "I was a classmate of Taft Churchill at Florida State for a short while."

"Oh, welcome, welcome!" I cheered, shouting for Gammy and Pastor Caldwell to join us.

I began introducing this stranger to everyone as if he were a part of me. My eyes were scanning for Nita. I was thinking that this might be just the man she had been looking for all those years. I had yet to find a single flaw.

"Any friend of Uncle Taft's is certainly a friend of ours." I smiled, offering my biggest welcome.

"Now, you know Taft is not here this weekend," I clarified.

"He is off on a cruise for two weeks with his company. You know he is lawyering in Orlando these days," I continued offering too much information.

"Is that right?" Chandler Monnier asked in his charming voice.

"That Taft was always a lucky guy," he said cheerfully.

"Luck has nothin' to do with it," Gammy chimed in. "My baby Taft is one of the hardest workers we have in the Churchill family," she said, pointing her finger toward Chandler.

"Ahh, I remember how fiery Taft said you can be," he said, giving Gammy a handsome smile.

"Well..." she said, slightly blushing.

"So, how can I reach Taft?" he asked.

I jotted down all of his contact numbers on the back of one of Cleeve's business cards and quietly handed it to him.

He went on to explain that he had dropped out of college after a year in Taft's class.

"School didn't come as easy for me as it did for Taft," he said humbly.

"Whatcha do for a livin'?" Gammy asked without hesitation.

"I do consulting work for a forensic research company based in New York. It's kind of a strange expertise but I enjoy it. Technological and scientific advancements have made our possibilities endless, Chandler continued enthusiastically. I must say, I have found my calling. The greatest part is that I can work from any location since so much of my research is done by computer. I travel to col-lect the data then work alone tying it all together and mak-ing correlations. I generally rent homes due to nature of my investigations. There is a tremendous amount of con-fidentiality associated with my locations."

At this, gammy leaned over to Pee-Paw and loudly whispered into his ear, "I'm figurin' he's FBI!" This was audible to all of us among the circle.

Surprisingly, you all have some fascinating psycholo-gists in your area that have assisted me with my work. I've had the opportunity to tap into their resources and they are more than willing to assist me with any of my questions. At this, he reeled off a few names casually. Among them, I caught the name Chapman. Gammy looked over and winked at me. She never missed a trick. I knew better than to mention Chapman being my doc because of all of those privacy laws.

He explained that he had lost touch with everyone from college. Chandler Monnier vaguely described a bad relationship. Apparently, this was the turning point for him to move and start over again. Suddenly, I had a mental image of Nita in her white bridal gown walking down the isle.

Gammy gave him a squint-eyed once-over, and then offered, "Well, we are delighted to have ya here, young man. Are you a Baptist?"

"Gammy!" I screamed.

She shot me a glance and then an innocent smile came about her face.

"Chandler, you will learn that I ask what I want to know and expect you to do the same. I mean no harm and hope you don't take any," Gammy said directly to the man.

"Umm, well...I have to be honest, Mrs. Churchill," he said kissing her hand as she giggled, nervously glancing at Pee-Paw.

"I have had some difficult times. To tell the truth, my faith needs some recharging, and I remembered Taft's love for this church and thought it might be just what I needed. It's only a forty-minute ride here and I just thought I would give it a try this week."

Gammy looked over at Mama, and in unison they chanted, "Praise God!"

Gammy continued, "Well, then, we will expect to see you here Wednesday evenin' around six, right?"

Poor ol' Chandler looked at me as if he was a plucked turkey, and I shrugged my shoulders, grinning.

Chapter 19

MY BEST FRIEND NITA LEDBETTER

Nita had been running around playing chase with Wit after the church luncheon. This was one of their common church yard games. If she caught him, she would drag him to the water's edge. There they would wrestle to see which one could force the other to get into the water in their clothes. My Wit lovingly called her his Aunt Nita because she felt like blood kin to us all. They would use me as their barrier to hide from one another before running back out making sprints across the back of the grounds. It tickled me to watch her running around in her church skirt. She had parted with her shoes revealing bare feet as filthy as Wit's. Her dark hair had fallen down and strands were now sticking to her sweaty face and neck. The older Nita got the more she resembled her daddy. She had become somewhat striking in a natural way.

At one point, I noticed Nita's father watching her curiously. He smiled finding amusement in his daughter's sense of freedom. That freedom had not always been there. A weight had been lifted from my dear friend but she didn't confide in me about the details.

She and Wit ran up to get lemonade from the ice-chest when Nita nudged me, calling my attention to Chandler Monnier seated at the picnic table with all of the other men.

Together, she and I watched Chandler.

"Nita, if you don't see somethin' delicious in that man I will tie you to the hood of my car Tuesday morning and take you to my head doctor," I teased.

"I'm about to give up on men."

"Don't ever tell me that Nita Ledbetter."

We were sipping our iced tea when Nita looked at me with the severity of an undertaker.

"I'm just not the kind of person that sees marriage as a good thing. I am workin' through it Caroline."

Then, there were only the sounds of clinking ice in our glasses. This was the rhythm of our friendship. We would likely kill for one another but when each of us got to a certain point of admitting to weakness, yield signs would go up. Assumptions were made that the other one would find offense in us diving in too deep. It was out of respect we allowed the limits.

I knew that her childhood had most likely been fraught with plenty of the same hell I had been subjected to the night of her party. There was no telling what had gone on in that house. I had always found my best friend's family to have a confidentiality clause of sorts similar to mine with my head doctor.

My mind shuffled back to Nita and me in grade school shortly after Jackson's death. We were playing on the monkey bars at Culley Elementary when that mean-assed Babs Paxton started teasing me. She was yelling something about my brother and Uncle Taft being gay. She said that's why Jackson was murdered.

Babs, who we privately nicknamed Baboon Ass, weighed about 190 lbs in the 5th grade and was from one of the family's that we strongly suspected inbreeding for generations. Even gammy referred to them as Pure D white trash without even following the comment with a Bible verse.

My panic attack started, causing me to hyperventilate right there by the monkey bars. I grabbed the bar leaning over gasping for air. Babs found humor in my drama.

It was then that ol' Babs delivered the unforgivable insult.

"Oh, look at Caroline havin' a mental attack. She can't breathe." She glanced over to her brood of butchy friends. I guess she's gonna end up as crazy as that mama of hers! The Churchills have ended up bein' queer and crazy."

Nita, who was a pint-sized child ran up to Babs and shoved her to the ground without thinking of the massive difference in their sizes. To her credit, she had caught the old baboon ass off guard.

She stood up and screamed, "You know it's true Nita Ledbetter!" Why don't you tell her what everybody says?"

Nita looked at me as tears welled in her eyes. She and I shared the unspoken fear that Babs could take her out in one punch.

"Her brother protected her Uncle Taft cause he was a queer too! Tell her Nita Ledbetter!"

It was then that a circle of the playground kids formed around them. The redneck girls were chanting... "Babs! Babs! Babs!"

My friend Sissy had handed me her brown lunch bag for me to breathe. I looked around and saw the teachers assembled at their picnic table gossiping. They had no idea about the scene transpiring at the monkey bars behind the big old oak tree.

Once I looked up again, my eyes met Nita's. Reaching deep inside myself; I found the urge to start a chant for her. Now, both names were being shouted in a chantlike battle.

It was then that Nita took her little toothpick body and walked up to that mean ol' Baboon-Ass and socked her in the nose.

Bab's enormous body landed in the sand with a thud. Her ratty ponytail made a violent slap onto her round face. The fat seemed to fall onto her bones seconds after the bulk of her body hit. Blood shot out of her nose onto her Copenhagen T-shirt.

"I'm gonna kill you Nita Ledbetter!"

It was then I spun back into present day thought. Nita was giggling watching the men at the table in front of us. She pointed calling my attention to them again. Cleeve, Daddy, Skeeter, and Double Barrel surrounded Chandler now. Later, even Alfred Ledbetter had joined in their conversation. They were asking him questions, and then the circle of men would burst into laughter. It seems that Mr. Chandler Monnier had been accepted on behalf of Uncle Taft.

Chapter 20

WHO IS ALFRED LEDBETTER?
2001

After the luncheon I stayed to clean up the dishes in the back of the church. That's when I heard a noise. All the other girls had gone and I was to lock up. Pastor Caldwell was in his office waiting for me. He would walk me to my car and help me carry the rest of my serving plates.

"Pastor Caldwell!" I yelled, questioning who might be there.

I walked out in the dining area and there stood Alfred Ledbetter. He looked embarrassed, as if he didn't know where he was.

It was then he asked if he could speak with me. We sat down, and he just played with his long fingernails for a few minutes. My patience was running thin 'cause I wanted to finish up and go home.

"Caroline," he started, "I know you have never thought much of me, but your family has made quite an impression on my life."

"Is that right, Mr. Ledbetter?" I asked curiously.

"I know that your brother went missing the night you were staying at our home. I found out about it and something happened to me that day. I feel that I need to explain," he continued.

"Mr. Ledbetter, you don't owe me an explanation," I said. "It was so long ago, really."

"Please call me Alfred, OK?

"Caroline, I never used to fit in back home. Kids teased me and never included me in anything. It has meant the world to me that you and Nita have always had one another. She never had to feel alone like me. You two have looked after one another and it warms my heart."

He looked down shamefully for a moment before returning his face to mine.

"I had started noticing that this was happening to my son, Ustus, about the time of the sleepover," he explained.

"Your brother was always nice to Ustus. The day he went missing he had even invited him on a fishing trip. I had been working so hard I had not been paying attention. One day I opened my eyes and saw my son struggling to find his place."

He paused as if he might cry.

"I was angry with myself and I had started to take it out on my family. It was never their fault," he said.

"For many years I have observed your family and seen how you handled your brother's passing. It has fascinated me."

"As I told you before, when my brother died, my mother lost her mind. We had to commit her in an asylum. It was the most awful place. I watched you and your father help your mother. You accepted her for what she could handle and made it comfortable. I admire that so much. My therapist calls it unconditional love," he said.

"My father must not have known of it. He left us with an aunt who was never around. I was essentially abandoned," he said this shamefully.

"I held anger inside of my heart for so long over my misfortunes.

"Something good came from your brother's death for me," he said. "I learned to appreciate my family again.

"It changed my life in a positive way somehow. I saw the mirror image of myself and my anger. I was becoming my father. By this I mean not showing my family the love they needed, and they were starting to fall apart," he explained.

Alfred Ledbetter started to stand as he said, "I don't know if this makes any difference to you, but I felt the need to tell you. Maybe now you won't see me as the monster I was becoming but instead as someone who has changed for the better," he said shyly.

I stood there with a man who I had not felt much for since childhood. We both had streams of tears running from our eyes. I reached over and hugged him.

"I am proud of you, Mr. Ledbetter...umm, Alfred," I quickly corrected myself.

Ustus had gone to college and he was an accountant in the city. He had married and had two daughters. I asked Mr. Ledbetter about them to give him a chance to talk about something happy before he left.

As he exited, I noticed that Pastor Caldwell had been standing in the back of the room. He walked over to me.

"Wonders never cease, do they, Caroline?" he said, laughing.

I had always adored Pastor Caldwell because he and Toot weren't from Culley and I knew that at times we must have all seemed half crazy to those poor people. I knew that there had to have been times that they wondered about our sanity.

Toot will sit right there at the dinner table with my mama and go along with her story about my brother. She never so much as makes a sideways expression. They understood without judgment that we were who we were.

I knew what Pastor was thinking at that minute, but didn't know how to bring it up. I hoped he would because it needed to be shared.

You see, shortly after Jackson's death, he and Toot spent a lot of time at our house. There were days they would help with my homework or drive me into town for my therapy. This was during the time Mama was so fond of the nerve pills. She would stay in bed all day most days back then.

Toot was concerned about me, and I knew Gammy had discussed everything with her at length. I told her and Pastor that I didn't like Mr. Ledbetter. I even told them about what I had seen at their house.

We prayed about it, and Daddy was informed. I watched Pastor Caldwell keep a close eye on the Ledbetter family for them and the rest of us. He was our protector and took the job rather seriously.

Naturally, at one time it crossed all of our minds that Alfred could have been the one that hurt Jackson. After all, Jackson himself had not felt easy about either of the Ledbetter men. I could tell in Pastor's eyes that the thought had crossed his mind, although he never said it.

Not long afterward, Alfred Ledbetter had joined the church. I know that I always wondered why he did this so shortly after our tragedy. Now it all made a lot more sense.

I could tell Pastor was as relieved as I was that night. "You see, Caroline," he had said, "there is good in this world. May I use a scripture now for us to think about for a few days?"

He started, "Galatians 2:20: *I have been crucified with Christ; it is no longer I who live, but Christ lives in me; and the life which I now live in the flesh I live by faith in the Son of God, who loved me and gave Himself for me.*"

Chapter 21

WIT FINDS TREASURE
2001

Cleeve and I had just sat down for our evening coffee and banana pudding when Wit ran inside the house, screamin' like a fool.

"Mama! Mama!" he yelped.

"Child, what on God's green earth is your problem?" I asked, walking into the living room.

"Look!" he shouted, far beyond control at this point.

I focused on the dirty box with teeth marks up and down the sides of it. It was then I noticed Tripod's excited yelps as he jumped up at Wit's hand holding the box. I remembered that fool dog digging it up the day before.

"Oh, Wit, I saw poor old Tripod dig that old thang up the other day," I explained. "I thought it was yours and figured it would get interestin' around here. It wasn't yours, though, was it?" I asked.

"*No!*" he said, almost out of breath.

"Was it Uncle Jackson's, Mama?" he asked.

"Pee-Paw told me that Uncle Jackson and Taft used to play over at the Baileys' all the time. He said the driftwood looked like a piece they played with a long time ago."

Cleeve placed his arm around my shoulder.

"No, no," I said, letting Cleeve know it wasn't Jackson's box. I could see him physically exhale out of relief, predicting the potential for Scarlett O'Hara style theatrics.

"Jackson specifically told me that he had a shark on the top of his." I explained. "Also, Jackson would have never hidden his box there because back then the water table was different. It would have been submerged."

"Well, then whose was this?" Wit asked in a disappointed voice.

"Honey, I don't know," I said, reaching for it.

"Maybe this is just an old box from a scurvy pirate," I said, making a face.

Wit was not amused with me in the least.

Cleeve quietly giggled at my attempt at changing the seriousness of the situation.

I reached for it and looked over the old box. It looked like a version of the boxes Wit and I had, but it was larger and required an old-fashioned type of key. My mind raced to the key I had found in Jackson's jacket years before. I quickly dismissed the thought as I saw the shape was not at all right.

"How can we get it open, Mama?" Wit asked, wide-eyed.

"Well, let me think about it, honey," I said.

"First of all," I continued, "we don't even know if we should. Maybe it belongs to the Baileys. They had a tribe of young men they raised in their home. Perhaps they too had treasure boxes. Tell you what. I will ask the Baileys tomorrow and see if they recognize it. If not, you and I will crush it if we have to so we can see what is inside, OK?" I said, hoping for peace with my son.

That night, I couldn't sleep, as usual. If nightmares came down on me, I couldn't remember, but solid sleep never did. I finally gave in and headed out to the dock to think. I opened the bench seat plucking out my box from Jackson.

I thought of the past and wondered how my mother ever got through it all. Now that I too was a mother, I found it even more unimaginable. The fact that we have never known how it happened made it even worse. There was somehow a gap left open, and it complicated everything.

Whenever it came up, and it rarely did, Mama's response was always, "Don't ya'll dare put me through anything else about Jackson." She would literally shout. "I have a place for him in my mind and heart now that I can retreat until I see him with the Lord one day. If ya'll get me stirred up again, it may be sooner than you think, so drop it," she would say.

Mama needed to make it easier to accept and change the details if she needed. Once we brought in reality, she couldn't make up the parts of her story that made it easier. I understood it in a way because I also did some of it. For me lately, I felt closer to Jackson than ever. I saw him in my mind, urging me and warning me. Why? Maybe it was simply my way of going to another level of acceptance among family members who never had. I spent most of my dock time thinking about our family and how we all protected one another so much that we may have stopped ourselves from healing.

As the sun started shedding slight light on the water, I peeled off my nightclothes and dove off the dock. The water always felt so good to my body. The smell of the morning ocean water would always be a daily gift for me. Somehow, I had hidden so many things away in my mind that I felt I couldn't express myself completely. Jumping off my dock had become one of the triumphs in my silly life.

I didn't fear the water, the life within it, or my ability to swim. The good Lord didn't give me wings to fly so I tried to stay out of the sky. He did give me the ability to swim, so I figured it was natural.

I found comfort with my dock and the salt water that surrounded it at high tide. I could see Jackson smiling at me. He would encourage me to make it to the shore. He would be laughing at Mama's response to my swimming in my underwear and bra in public.

* * *

That morning, after Mama and Wit's typical departure I walked over to the Baileys'. Double Barrel was already out in his shed getting his next project lined up. I carried the old box in one hand and my coffee in the other.

"Mr. Bailey," I said, alerting him to my presence.

His cheerful head popped out, so excited to have company.

"Whatca got there, young lady?" he asked.

I began explaining about Tripod's find and Wit's stake in the treasure. Mr. Bailey was laughing with excitement.

"Those young'ins!" he said, laughing at the simple joy of kids.

He had no idea what it was or if it belonged to his kids or not.

All of them had been gone for years and visited regularly. He figured if they had ever had the box they were long over whatever they may have had in it.

"Wonder how I can get into it?" I asked.

He turned around without thinking twice and grabbed his huge mallet from the alligator board wall in his shed.

In one thrust, he hit the old wooden box and it was done.

"There!" he said, glad to feel useful.

I squatted down and immediately recognized the handwriting on some of the cards in the box. The box was insulated with some sort of tarp material. Although the outside was shot, the inside was actually in great shape.

"You know, Mr. Bailey, I think I know exactly who this belongs to," I said.

I started sprinting back to my house. I could hear him saying something else in question form, but I was too excited for small talk.

I knew before arriving at my back door that this old treasure had once been Uncle Taft's. I was sure he had probably forgotten about it.

This would be fun. Too bad I couldn't call him now since he was on his fancy cruise. He would have lots of excitement from us when he returned, between his friend Chandler coming to fellowship with us and my finding his old box.

I returned to the house and took out any of the personal notes, leaving only rocks, marbles, and some Mira lures for Wit's entertainment. I, however, had an appointment on my dock to read the papers inside. I assumed they were old grade school nothingness notes. I figured they would give me ammunition to poke fun of Taft later.

I plopped down on my spot while opening the first of four notes. The first two appeared to be secret coordinates for scavenger hunts. I laughed out loud, thinking about my goofball uncle.

"No!" I giggled. I apparently found one of old Taft's grade school notes.

* * *

M.

I hope you will understand that I can't hang out with you anymore. I am still trying to figure out who I am. I'm sorry if you misunderstood anything I did or said. I think it's better if we just go our separate ways for now.

Please don't take this personally. I had a talk with my nephew and he convinced me that this is the right choice for now. Funny, how sometimes you find wisdom in those younger than you.

Please take care of yourself. I will be at my parents' house this weekend so please don't try and reach me.

Thanks for understanding
Good luck with everything
T.

Finally, I read the last one.

Jackson,

Man, I don't know where to start. First, I am sorry that I jumped all over you the other day. You know that I was just confused and I probably never should have even talked to you about it. I am older than you so I shouldn't worry you with it.

I listened to you, Jackson. The note was left a few hours ago and I feel good about it. Thanks for your advice. BE TRUE TO YOURSELF...

Your Uncle and Friend,
Taft

Chapter 22

BUMP IN THE NIGHT
2001

That Wednesday, we were thrilled to see Chandler sitting in one of the pews well before service time. He was reading a book about renewing spirituality. Gammy walked in and started right over to him.

"Why, look at you, young man," Gammy said. "Aren't you a bright shinin' star set on fire with the good book?" she said.

"Hi, Mrs. Churchill," Chandler said in a timid voice.

Gammy grabbed his book and started fanning through it.

"Make sure there ain't none of that interpretation of the Lord's word in this book, child," Gammy warned. "If you need any spiritual guidance you come over to see me or Buckley. Naturally, you should also see Smitty Caldwell."

Gammy continued, "He has been our pastor here since 1976. He started when he was just twenty-one."

At this, I was standing there motioning for Nita to come keep the new Baptist company at his pew.

Gammy couldn't hold her tongue.

"Well, here you go, granddaughter! We may just get Chandler to turn Baptist and find his wife right here in Culley Cove," she said.

Nita's face turned three shades of red.

Chandler joined us all for dinner at Pastor and Toot's house that night. Nita had been invited for the good of the order. He was such a gentleman. He ate with perfect manners. After dinner, he helped clear the table. Toot fussed, but he wouldn't have her doing it without his help.

While we were cleaning dishes, Nita took a phone call leaving me alone with Chandler for the first time

"You know, this is just what we need," I said. "If Taft's big-city life starts connecting with Culley Cove, he just may want to move back here after all," I continued, smiling at Chandler.

"Why did he leave?" he asked me while drying off a tea glass.

I wondered briefly if he knew anything about my Uncle's struggles with his orientation. Occasionally, that thought would pop into my head and I would rush it out as fast as it entered.

"Oh, well...Uncle Taft and my brother were very close, as you probably know," I said, hesitating.

"I can't remember," he said sheepishly as if he was trying to collect names in his mind.

"I often recognize names when I hear them, but it has been so long, I can't remember details," he explained.

"You see, Taft and I were in a band together for a while," he explained. "I know your gammy wasn't to know about it. I never knew what to mention after all of these years. We had some weird dudes join us at times. Did Taft ever mention any of the whacky band groupies to you?"

"No, I didn't realize Taft was in a band," I lied.

"I saw your daddy, uncles, and pee-paw a few times when they came out to watch us perform. They would watch but always leave before the performances ended. I think your family wanted this to be a phase your uncle was going through. I never ever officially met them. We were all kind of..." he paused, "well, hippies back then," he said, embarrassed.

"In those days, everybody was starting bands and studying free love," he explained.

"I never knew any of that!" I said excitedly.

"Well, anyway, sometimes I can't remember things cause in those days we were all crazy hippies and I'll leave it at that," he said, grinning at me, shaking his head.

"Now, back to your brother," Chandler said, redirecting our conversation.

"Well, my brother died in '78," I continued.

"Oh, I am so sorry. I shouldn't have..."

I interrupted his apology.

"He and Taft were really close and..." I felt the tears filling my eyes and stopped.

"Caroline, I am so sorry. I shouldn't have pried like that."

"No, no it's OK. I just still have trouble..." Again the tears came.

It was that moment I saw something in Chandler Monnier's expression that just didn't seem right. You know, when you get something new and your best friend fails to mention it? That generally means she's jealous, right? Well, Chandler's expression wasn't one of true regret. He didn't say or show enough somehow.

Finally, Chandler cheerfully said, "Well, that was about the best meal I have had since Sunday at that after service lunch you and Nita put on," he said.

I thought he lost interest in the topic of my brother and Taft until I saw him on the back porch having coffee with Pastor Caldwell. The pastor was explaining some of the circumstances of Jackson's death to Chandler. I figured he felt guilty for upsetting me in the kitchen and sought guidance from Pastor Caldwell at the time.

* * *

That evening, Jackson came to my dream world, motioning for me to follow him again.

In this dream, I could see him so clearly. He had on his red shirt and jeans. His hair was longer like the day he went missing. He was running ahead of me. I was trying to catch up.

He turned around and stopped, looking at me so seriously.

"Caroline, remember to be true to yourself. Trust yourself!" He said this over and over again.

Finally, I woke myself up, screaming, "*I hear you!*"

My body was covered in sweat. My hair was even wet. Somehow, Cleeve had managed to sleep through it all. I was burning up.

Here we go again. I was up and on my way to the dock. I lay on the plank that morning in the dark, staring at the sky. I kept thinking about Chandler. He didn't ask much about Taft. Every once in a while he would tell us a funny story from college, but he didn't seem to me to really know my uncle.

I would be glad when Uncle Taft called and told us more about Chandler Monnier. He was charming, but almost too charming to come to Culley. Most of the women here were married. The unmarried ones were in college, away. He was kind, and I was cruel for questioning him. He somehow seemed to know too much yet nothing at all about us.

I suppose I am turning into a skeptic, I thought as I moved my head onto Tripod's belly. The crazy dog's snores were

179

as loud as Cleeve's. Suddenly, he reared up and starting howling. He ran off the dock like a fool with those three legs getting tangled up with his fast pace.

Tripod stirred up the Bailey's bird dogs next door. Now we were in a full-blown bark-a-thon.

About that time, I heard a gunshot.

Cleeve ran out of the house with his hair standing up on his head. He looked both ways in a panic, between the sounds of the dogs and the gunshots.

The moon caught the reflection of Mr. Bailey holding his rifle. He was wearing only his boxers. He shot it again and again.

"Double Barrel!" I shouted.

"Caroline, we have a prowler, girl!" he said, sounding like a baby learning to speak. It was then I realized that he had his top denture plate out of his mouth. In all of the commotion, I suppose he only had time to grab his rifle.

By now, poor old Thyra had run out and started trying to cover her husband with a sheet. She had his missing dentures in the other hand.

"Crazy man!" she screeched. "Put something over yourself!" She was struggling to put his teeth in his mouth while still managing to hold the sheet over his boxers.

Once she got his teeth in, she starting bouncing between holding the sheet and touching her hair net. She never took the hair net off but seemed to feel that if she touched it somehow we wouldn't be able to see it.

Cleeve ran toward him asking what the Baileys had seen.

Double Barrel told us he had seen some crazy man running through the walking trail.

"Now that them trees is cut," he explained, "I can see everything like it's in a glass globe."

"The thug looked to be 'bout six feet tall," he continued. "He don't know how I got my nickname." Double Barrel snickered.

"He was dancin' around over there like a he was in an ant bed. He has good speed though. He was fast," he said, catching his breath.

All the while, poor Thyra held the sheet over her husband's boxers in embarrassment.

Double Barrel kept looking at her, enjoying her excitement. "Honey, if they see something they ain't seen before, they should shoot at it!" he said to his wife, chuckling.

"Old man, you gone give poor Cleeve and Caroline a heart attack," she reprimanded.

"She never thinks I see or hear anything!" Mr. Bailey explained behind her head.

Just then, the police arrived. Mr. Bailey started explaining what he saw. The police had their flashlights out and began their search.

"Hey, we found something!" one of the officers shouted.

His flashlight was pointing onto the rock at the water's edge. It was the spot where Jackson had died. There was an empty beer bottle there on the rock, standing up perfectly. The wrapping on the bottle was new and not weathered. The officers knew that this wasn't something Mr. Bailey would have had in his yard. You see, Double Barrel drank only whiskey and kept it hidden underneath his claw-foot tub. Everybody in town knew this because Thyra talked about it at the Culley Ladies Baptist Prayer Group Meets.

Still, he called Mr. Bailey over and asked if any of the workers could have had a beer on the property.

"Shoot, no! Not on my clock," Double Barrel said with certainty. Then he leaned over to the officer and whispered, "And I don't take to beer myself."

"It sure out looks like somebody was sitting right here on this old rock just enjoying themselves," the officer said. "Does anything appear to have been stolen?" the deputy asked.

We all did a quick once-over and reported that nothing was gone.

"Maybe it was just some teens out drinking beer. You know they have always made a target out of your house, Double Barrel," the officer said, remembering all of the toilet paper rolls from earlier years.

"Well, they needn't be comin' on my property to do the devil's work!" Mr. Bailey said defensively.

Chapter 23

MRS. MARSHALL
SERVES TEA
2001

I had told no one but cancelled my appointment with Dr. Chapman on Monday. He had helped me find my sea legs but now I wanted to fly alone to see how strong I had become. I received a call from Detective Osbourne, who said that Mrs. Marshall in Seaside would be willing to meet with me. She would only do it if the detective was present. He explained that she had become somewhat of a recluse since her son was murdered. It was getting much worse with age; she was skeptical of everyone.

She had kept in touch with Osbourne, who was dedicated to this case. He was determined to solve it, even as a cold case, before he retired.

I dressed as I knew Mama would think was proper that day. I wore a long church skirt with a matching headband and flat shoes. I wore only pearls for jewelry. Pearls were never overstated, Mama always said. I figured Mrs. Marshall was likely a churchgoing lady. Osbourne had told me enough that I gathered she had lots of old money.

"There's nothin' I would love more than to retire solving the first case I helped open," he said to me as he grabbed a folder from his desk.

Osbourne and I rode together to the Marshall home in Seaside proper. I was slightly concerned that Cleeve would get wind of me riding around Seaside with another man. He might think I was havin' an affair. Lord, can you imagine? Then Mama would find out what I was really doing. I don't know which scenario would be worse of the two.

Jackson was urging me. I could feel it. I didn't care about risks for the first time in my life since he left. Whether it was true that he was egging me on or if I just needed to believe it didn't matter to me anymore.

We approached the large, elegant home. The mailbox read "Marshall." The yard was perfectly manicured and the picket fence surrounding it was freshly painted.

Osbourne knocked on the door. There was no answer so he rang the bell. Finally, a housekeeper answered the door and asked us for our identification. Osbourne winked at me in jest.

After proving that we were, in fact, who we were supposed to be, we were escorted through a long, dignified hallway. At the end of it was a bright room surrounded by crystal-clear windows overlooking a large swimming pool with a waterfall. I knew Gammy would have one word for it: gaudy!

Mrs. Marshall sat on a silk sofa with a perfect silver tea set in front of her on a glass coffee table.

"Welcome," she said, encouraging our entry with a hand gesture.

"Please sit down wherever you are comfortable," she continued, giving us a pointed once-over.

The housekeeper offered us tea and poured it with the grace of a ballet dancer, which almost made me laugh.

"I am, as you know, Mrs. Francis Marshall. My son was abducted and murdered many years ago," she continued. "The tyrant has never been apprehended. I suspect you are aware of all of this," she said in a matter-of-fact tone.

"Why yes," I said respectfully.

Before I could speak again, she interrupted.

"Frankly, I am rather surprised at your interest, my dear. Many years ago I contacted your mother on a number of occasions and she was not at all polite with me. She seemed to want to just forget how our sons were murdered," she said in a very curious tone.

"I'm afraid mama has never accepted my brother's death," I attempted to explain.

"Actually, she had accepted the death itself, but she refuses to come to terms that he died the way he did. She never wanted it discussed. She likes to pretend that he died in his sleep because it makes it easier for her to comprehend," I explained, grasping for words that would fit.

"Umm mmmn, I see," she said, looking at me as if I was straight out of an institution for the mentally deranged.

I suddenly felt defensive of mama. If anybody was gonna criticize her, it would be me. I loved her and that made it OK.

"Please don't misunderstand me, Mrs. Marshall," I said hopefully.

"My mama is a smart lady. This has just been... well..." I paused, as words weren't coming to me.

Tears had started to fill my eyes, and Mrs. Marshall noticed it.

"I know. I know," Mrs. Marshall said sympathetically.

She was all too aware of trying to blink tears away before they sprinkled down your face.

"It changes you, doesn't it, dear?" she said.

"More than I can ever explain to anyone," I said as I was feeling our connection.

"Well, Caroline. May I call you Caroline?" she asked with a kind smile.

"Yes," I replied wide-eyed.

"Caroline, I must say I am curious. What has made you override your mother in this situation after all of these years?" she asked.

"To be honest, I have had nightmares since the night after Jackson died. I have had lots of issues with independence and overprotecting my own son. As a result, I have been seeing a therapist since grade school behind Mama's back."

I paused. "And for most of my adult life with her superficial approval," I explained, feeling like a child.

Mrs. Marshall was shaking her head, indicating that she understood.

"I have come to a place in my grief or maturity, whichever it is, where I simply need to know more. I carry some guilt that has been in my soul for way too long."

I had to pause to swallow. My mouth was dry.

"You see, I encouraged my brother to come home early from camp that summer," I explained. "Otherwise he wouldn't have even been home," I said, feeling embarrassed to disclose so much to a stranger.

"Caroline, I too carry guilt. I am the reason that my Ted came home from Miami that weekend. I had asked him to come and talk some sense into my younger son, Danny. He was attending Clemson and making terrific progress. He suddenly decided that he wanted to stop it and study music with a band. Can you imagine?" She asked shaking her head.

"I had just had a horrendous argument with him about it. I was determined that he would go to medical school as my husband had done, she said proudly.

"Ted came here to talk Danny out of changing his major. Oh, Danny wanted to pursue rock music at the time. He stood right over there," she said while gesturing to the rug.

"He told me that he was talented and that I was not letting him think for himself," Mrs. Marshall explained. "He said that I wasn't allowing him to be free. Truth is, I was going to have him move home if he pursued this rock and roll music foolishness."

She stopped then, glancing into her teacup.

"Poor Ted took the time to discuss it with his young brother just as I had asked."

Now she leaned forward and whispered, "Danny was a little different."

"This so called band was the only thing that ever made him feel included according to Ted."

I could feel pricks of my memories about my conversation with Uncle Taft when she used the word different. Those were thoughts that were not allowed.

Mrs. Marshall started, "Danny took Ted's advice and called his band buddies to tell them to count him out. One of the boys was furious with Danny, and Ted got on the phone with him and asked him to back off his brother.

"After that, Danny got right back on track and continued to study medicine. Today he practices in DC, you know," she said as she placed her cup into the saucer.

"Do you remember who his friend was in the band?" I asked, wondering if it was Chandler Monnier.

"Yes, his name was Max," she said. "I remember thinking that was a name for a dog, not a boy," she continued shaking her head, still disapproving.

I thought to myself how childish I had been to even ask the name.

Detective Osbourne had been out of the room. He reentered, apologizing for taking a call.

Mrs. Marshall looked up at him.

"Oh, we are having a lovely talk," she told him, smiling.

"I wish I had contacted Caroline a long time ago rather than her mother," she continued, almost insulting me.

"Please understand Mama," I explained. "She loved Jackson so much. She just can't face it."

"I know. I am not angry with her, but I needed someone to talk to," Mrs. Marshall said sincerely. "I felt so alone. My husband, Gordon, discussed it only in terms of suing everybody for everything he could think of at the time. He has Alzheimer's now and is in a facility," she said, looking down sadly.

Osbourne now explained his dead end.

"As you know these cases had similarities in the way the bodies were found. We looked for something to connect the dots but never found anything except the necklaces and..." his voice trailed off.

"What was it?" I asked.

"You don't know?" Mrs. Marshall asked in a screechy voice, holding her pinky out while grasping her teacup.

"No," I said. "Mama has never let me know anything."

He continued, "Each of these bodies had a wire necklace with a paper sign saying the same lines.

"BE TRUE TO YOURSELF AND GIVE THAT GIFT TO YOUR LOVED ONES.

"The writing was so incredibly small that it took magnifying glasses to make out the words," Osbourne continued.

"Then there was the other part", Osbourne said "The boys' pants were shredded."

My face was turning red. The tears were coming and I couldn't stop them. Was Jackson's murderer gay? I didn't want to know anymore. This must have been mama's big secret. Had everyone feared a secret worse to them than murder itself?

"What is it, dear?" Mrs. Marshall asked, noticing my face.

"Jackson," I said, "Jackson used to say that to me all the time. He told me a guidance counselor had said it to him once and he liked it."

I had to stop and collect myself so I could talk without my voice breaking. I wasn't going to even address the shredded pants. I would focus on the necklace.

I continued, "He would say only the first part. *Be true to yourself.* He didn't include the last part," I said, crying into my hands.

"Now, now," Mrs. Marshall said. "Please don't cry."

"My Danny had said that a great deal as well," she said thoughtfully. "I asked him where he heard it when the necklace was found on his brother's body."

"I knew that unsightly necklace was nothing that belonged to Ted," she said as if she were disgusted by the very thought of it.

"Danny said it was something a few of the boys at Clemson were saying all of the time," Mrs. Marshall explained. "You have to remember that this was the seventies and all of that hippie truth, freedom nonsense was running wild," Mrs. Marshall explained.

Finally, I asked the big question sounding more like my mother than I wanted to.

"Mrs. Marshall, did Danny date much?"

She tilted her head back and in a half smile and said, "The girls here never suited his taste."

My mind raced connecting the possibility of her son being gay and how that just may connect with our family. I needed to move the conversation in a different direction and fast. I should keep the focus on the necklaces.

* * *

After my meeting with Mrs. Marshall, Osbourne drove me back to the station. I heard him on the phone arguing about some missing case files. He hung up the phone and looked over at me.

"Rookies!" he said in an irritated tone.

"They can't ever be where they are supposed to be," he ranted. "The very moment you don't need them they want to call you and ask you about everything you are doing. I have this one new fellow that is bugging me to death!" He said in an irritated grunt.

After he brushed it off, he looked over at me and asked, "So, did you get anything useful out of that?"

"Well, I am stunned over the necklaces, I must say," I said honestly. "Did you see if you could track the wire manufacturer to find out where they were purchased?" I asked.

"Oh, that is very Nancy Drew of you, Caroline," he said, smiling over at me.

"Yeah," Osbourne continued, "we checked stores locally and even later factories. These particular necklaces had special strings. They were almost like guitar strings, to be honest. Those were intertwined with a wire to give them more strength. We figure that this nut job must have done it himself. The writing on the paper sign he attached was in a type of boxy print. It was as if he was trying to show the words in a whisper voice, if that makes any sense."

He then said to me honestly, "I tell you, this case has worn my brain down to grits.

"I am so embarrassed that we have as little as we do. It has sure put a label of Barney Fife on my head over the years," he admitted humbly.

"I have looked over all of the evidence more than anyone and I tell you there just aren't enough pieces. This comes back to our discussion when you first came into my office. Whoever it is must be is an intelligent egomaniac. He calculated every single thing he did right down to the necklaces.

"He probably has some major point to be made based on his fantasy world. Remember, he won't likely think rules apply to him," he said as he glanced over at me.

"Between us, the guy was most likely gay. He didn't molest the young men but he did try to humiliate them by shredding their pants. It had to mean something crazy.

I could feel the shock waves of adrenaline flowing through my spine.

"Are you sure there aren't other cases with similar evidence far off that we don't know about?" I asked.

"You can't ever know for sure," Osbourne said. "It ain't like the movies when you are solving a case."

He was hesitant and then said, "There was one other case about that wealthy doctor. We never could figure if we had a copycat or if the cases were actually related."

"Can you tell me about it?" I asked.

"Two years after your brother's death, the body of an older retired doctor was found in his mansion. It was way up in Seaside Trellis. That is a good two hundred miles from here, you know," he continued. That's the ritzy area where all the rich people live. We don't know the law enforcement over there and they weren't impressed with us down in the sticks."

"The old doc was a widow and had one son who was in college at the time. That boy had a falling out with his dad and they hadn't spoken for a few years. The poor kid hadn't been able to get his dad by phone for days. Apparently, the boy was a geeky sort of weirdo like his dad. The housekeeper says the old man had fired her and mailed her a check to close out her pay," he said.

"The sad part is until the old guy's son decided that he was seriously concerned about dear ol' dad, two years had passed," he explained. "The kid called the police in Seaside Trellis and they went over and found the man. Coroner suspects the time of death to be two years before."

"Talk about guilt," he said, glancing over at me.

"How terrible," I said, amazed at the story.

"Maybe I missed something, but how is this case even remotely similar to Jackson and the Marshall kid?" I asked, puzzled.

"Oh, yeah, I left out that part, didn't I?" he said, crossing his eyes at me.

"On the mirror in the old man's bedroom, that same slogan was written in crayon," Osbourne went on. "You know, the same saying that was on the other two urrr..." he stopped.

"Bodies?" I finished the sentence for him.

"You got it," he confirmed.

"So no necklaces and it was an old man?" Maybe the killer just wanted to steal from the doctor." Osbourne said.

"We didn't know if anything was gone or not. The doctor had neither friends nor family except for the son. It was pretty obvious they weren't close. Certain high-ticket items that carried insurance were still in the home. Lord knows what else was in there before the body was found."

As the drive continued Osbourne cut the silence. "I will never forget you standing there at your Grandma Churchill's house when we would go ask questions. You always looked like you wanted to talk to us," he reflected, turning into the courthouse.

"Your Mama Shug is a pistol herself though," he said reflectively. "She always made a point to offer us food, but kindly shut us up," he said, smiling just thinking of it.

"That's about the nicest way we have ever been told to buzz off in our careers," he said, glancing over at me.

We filled the remainder of our drive back with small talk. I tried to concentrate but my mind was with Jackson and Mrs. Marshall. There was so much to decipher.

Once we reached the courthouse, I got straight into my car to head out for Culley. I had new information and I needed to let it marinate in my brain for a while.

Chapter 24

MY NEW ACCOMPLICE
2001

As I drove home, I was feeling guilty about going behind Mama's back on this. She would skin my hide, old as I was. If she caught me, I would have to remind her that she had pushed me back into therapy as an adult. This was after she watched a documentary about siblings of murdered children killing themselves.

I decided to leave a message for Uncle Taft. He of all people could understand my interest in finding closure. Maybe as a prosecutor he would even want to help me dig deeper.

I knew he wouldn't be back from his cruise, but I hoped that I could at least leave him a message and he might check in when they docked and return my call. My message was long-winded as usual. I always hate voice mail 'cause they are designed for quick speakers. I always try to talk as fast as I can to get as much on there as possible.

Once the voice mail indicator light went on...I was off talking one hundred miles an hour. I explained about Chandler Monnier worshipping in Culley. I went on explaining that Gammy and I were going to set up him and Nita. Then I briefly said that I needed to talk to him as soon as he could call me. I was working on something interesting. I would have said more, but the damn voice mail cut me off.

It took Taft a few days, but finally he returned my call when he got to a land site on his cruise.

He reported that he was tanned and handsome. His voice had gotten higher pitched through the years. He talked to me like many of my girlfriends did. I loved it but sometimes it still made me giggle.

He then went onto to tell me what a great guy Chandler was back in school. He was one of the first friends Taft had made on campus. His tone then got more serious as he told me about Chandler being in the band with that crazy guy.

"So, this Chandler is OK then, huh, Uncle? I asked.

"One hundred percent, Caroline," Taft confirmed.

"Oh, yeah!" My old three-legged dog dug up your treasure box!" I said.

"No kidding?" Taft said.

"Did ya'll drive over to the old fishing docks? Gosh, I thought that part of the marina was closed down," he asked curiously.

"What?" I asked. "Tripod found it on the Baileys' property. Bailey has cleared the land there," I explained.

There was silence on the phone.

"Taft? Are you still there?"

"Caroline, somebody else must have dug up that thing and your old dog found it."

"Taft, I don't much care. I found some of your love notes in it. You were letting that one girl off real easy. You mentioned even taking my sweet brother's advice," I teased.

"Then of course there was the letter you wrote to Jackson and I will save it for you in case you want that, Taft," I changed my voice to serious now.

"Caroline, it's really important that you keep that entire box for me to look over when I come home," he said.

"Well, I'll be in Culley next weekend. Be sure to let Gammy know for me, OK?" he said.

His voice seemed troubled.

I thought I might have angered him going through the old box. I suddenly felt awkward.

I quickly thought about the band and how much fun it might be to tease my uncle about it, but then thought better of it after noticing he was acting a little strangely.

That evening, Wit and I were helping Gammy pick peas out of her garden. I started asking questions about how she had been able to handle Jackson's death the way she did.

"Gammy, you are such a strong person," I said, squatting down to detach a pea from its stem.

"I remember your initial response was to find out who did it and punish them. How did you get past it, Gammy?"

"Caroline Churchill Burton, your mama would have our heads on a silver platter right now if she knew we were even entertainin' this conversation." She stopped working and just sat down in the dirt between two rows of peas.

I plunked down beside her, hollering over to Wit. "Go inside, son, and check on Pee-Paw, would you?"

"Granddaughter, one thing you learn in a big family is that you have to respect each other.

"Sometimes you may not agree with em', but you line up what's most important and go with it," Gammy explained, wiping the sweat off her brow with her floral handkerchief.

"Yeah, it took everything in me not to race around and find that miserable asshole," Gammy shot the word out, instantly moving her hand to cover her lips.

Quickly, she closed her eyes and whispered, "Proverbs 25:28 - "Like a city whose walls are broken down is a man who lacks self-control."

"I'm sorry, Caroline, but I get so cussed mad," she said.

"Gammy, I know. I do too. It's funny; I feel more of a need to know today than I had before. I can't explain it," I said drawing in the sand with my finger like a child.

Gammy gazed at me for a long while; she was processing.

"We handled this the way your mama needed us to. She still had you to raise and we needed her to keep her mind. I wondered for a while if she would, though; she struggled. Lord, that woman had it rough," Gammy said, shaking her head.

"Buckley and I talked many a night about how us sweeping it away would work on your head, Caroline," Gammy explained, looking at me seriously.

"Did we mess you up?" she asked.

I looked up at her and laughed.

"Gammy, you didn't do any more harm than was already done with me bein' born a Churchill," I said, still smiling at her.

Gammy gave me a look of understanding that I found in her eyes.

"Somethin' just doesn't smell right to me about the whole thing and never did," Gammy said.

She continued, "Who knew Jackson would be coming home? Just the church, right?" she said, "Would that crazy no-good have just killed anybody or was it intended to be Jackson?" Gammy said in her determined voice that bordered on evangelic intonation.

"I know, Gammy," I agreed. "They had to be here that day, waiting, right? Maybe Jackson walked up on something that he wasn't supposed to see and they couldn't let him tell," I said.

Gammy was nodding her head in agreement.

"Gammy, I want to tell you something. If I do, you have to promise me you won't tell anybody else, though. Mama would kill me," I whispered.

My grandmother's eyes were wide open. She shook her head in quiet agreement as she put her big bucket of peas down beside her.

Gammy leaned forward and explained, "I am your grandmother, and you are my blood. I won't ever breathe a word of it without your permission."

I paused, just collecting my thoughts. I was searching for a way to present the facts without upsetting her.

"Do you remember the policeman who was assisting at the detective's office with Jackson's case?" I asked.

"Osbourne!" Gammy shouted, answering as if it were a *Wheel of Fortune* question.

"Yeah," I continued, "I've been meeting with him about Jackson and the other boy who went missing over in Seaside."

At this, Gammy's face was completely still as if she might be going into a state of shock.

"God in heaven, Sugar Churchill is gon' beat you and me both, child," she said now, closing her eyes and looking to heaven.

"I know, Gammy," I said in shame. "I had to start looking into it.

"My doctor," I said pointing to my head to specify his specialty.

At this, Gammy rolled her eyes.

"He has had me searching my mind to find out how to deal with it all and..."

Gammy cut me off. "Good Lord, whatever you do don't tell anybody that's what gotcha going on about this. They will send you straight to the crazy house, granddaughter," she warned.

Gammy was as sharp as a tack and I knew that she, like me, had memorized the name of the other boy whose case was similar.

"I met with Mrs. Marshall in Seaside Paradise the other day, Gammy," I said, slowly waiting for her response.

At this, Gammy dramatically fell back into the dirt and just stared at the sky.

Then she said, "It's about to get shore nuff interestin' around here. Lord in heaven," she said now, trying to sit back up.

"What did she say?" Gammy asked curiously, squinting her eyes to taste every word.

It was then I told my gammy about the necklaces as I brushed the dirt out of her hair. I reminded her how Jackson said that same line over and over that particular summer. Gammy remembered it as I had.

She reminded me that Taft had gotten into saying that too. She assumed he got it from Jackson.

"Maybe it came from somebody none of us know," Gammy said.

"Ummm, granddaughter. You suspect that there are lots of thangs we haven't figured in to this mess, don't ya?" Gammy asked with an eager expression on her face.

"Caroline, I will never try to go against your Mama's wishes 'cause I know she has had to deal with this in her own way. I love your mama like I gave birth to her myself," Gammy was easing into this carefully. "Your Mama's mama was my dearest friend on this earth and I am dedicated to her."

Gammy paused for a moment and tears filled her blue eyes. She let them dry before looking back at me.

"The very idea of some old cussed ass coming over here..." She halted midsentence, putting her hand over her mouth as if it would extract the nasty word from the air.

After a deep breath, Gammy started again. "The idea of that evil thang comin' over here to our very own Culley and taking Jackson from us was bad enough. Then your mama, God love her, trying to brainwash us all into believin' he passed over in a quiet sleep has just 'bout killed me, Caroline," Gammy said with her determined voice.

"We figured we had to help out Mama Shug the best we could. Lord, your uncles were ready to go out on a killin' spree for sure. Thyra stuck with me to keep Double Barrel and my boys from ended up in prison. Skeeter wanted to pursue it. I had to call a meeting without your mama and daddy and tell all of 'em to back off it for your mama's sake.

"I told them that if Shug went to the loony bin she couldn't raise you right. It took Toot and me two years to get her to act anywhere near clearheaded," Gammy continued.

"Now, all that said, what we gone do?" Gammy asked with the excitement of a schoolgirl.

I explained my relationship with Osbourne. Then told her my thoughts about Mama, and about how my therapist had been encouraging me to explore my mind more on the subject.

"Granddaughter, I ain't gon' to mince words with ya," she said, big-eyed. "I have never had much respect for people that make a livin' nosin' around in other people's business. It sure seems to me that if somebody is fool enough to get into that mess, they had a head problem their own self," she said, pointing her finger at me.

"I know, Gammy, and regardless of how I came to make the decision to move forward, I have," I explained. "Can we agree on that?" I asked.

"Yes, ma'am," she said, smiling at me as if we were conspiring to smuggle immigrants over US lines.

"I would very much like for you to go over and meet Mrs. Marshall with me. She is so nice, Gammy. She really is lonely, and like us, she has thought through so many small details.

"Maybe together we can all come up with some ideas about why or if these cases are even related.

"That necklace has been a telling sign to me, Gammy," I said, hearing the determination in my own voice.

"Jackson said that to me all the time," I said, feeling the tears fill in my eyes.

Gammy leaned over toward me now.

"Child, let's get them peas inside before Buckley comes out here thinking I've died in the garden,"
Gammy said. "This here conversation is between us.
You set up whatever meetin' you need, and I will find a
way to go with you."

She started walking then stopped to look at me
seriously. "Now let's be careful we ain't flat out lyin' to
nobody, but we tell a story that has some kind of truth to
it, OK?" Gammy said as she winked at me, grasping her
pea bowl and then marching toward the house.

So now I had an accomplice.

Chapter 25

UNWITTINGLY, I ANGER HIM
2001

The next morning, I drove into the city and met with Dr. Chapman. I told him that he had inspired me to move forward. He warned me that even if I ever solved the case, it wouldn't bring Jackson back.

I thanked him for helping me find the strength inside myself. I explained that Gammy wouldn't work as well with me if I kept referencing what she referred to as a head doctor.

After that meeting, I went to the courthouse unannounced. I took the stairs for exercise up to the second floor to see if Osbourne was in.

"Well, Nancy Drew, aren't you on fire these days?" he said.

I explained that Gammy was on board with me.

"Lord, dissention in the Churchill family!" he said, amused.

"Mama just can't handle it, but that doesn't mean we can't," I said.

"Look, maybe nothing comes of it, but for me, just knowing I tried helps my conscience. Does that make sense?" I asked.

"Absolutely," Osbourne said sympathetically.

* * *

He watched every detail of the conversation from his cubicle. He pretended to be looking into his computer screen. He carefully burrowed his head down but his eyes were cut up to observe.

He ran into the restroom and splashed water on his face. All color was leaving him as he went numb. His hate was rising. He got a paper towel to dry his face before glaring at the mirror.

Looking at his reflection, he said in his whisper-light voice, *"Oh, Caroline, how disappointed they will be when they find your body.*

"Ummm, where should they find you?

"Maybe out on your dock during an early morning therapy session with yourself.

"Oh, she is so brave that she jumps off the dock into the water." He laughed.

"*Is that how you fight your evil fears of how Jackson died? Me?*" He found humor in this very fact.

"*I will throw you off that dock and we will see how fearless you are then.*" He fixed his hair as he grinned into the mirror.

He laughed back at himself. He then wiped his face once more before forcing a smile and walking back out into the courthouse.

Chapter 26

TAFT IS UNSETTLED
2001

Taft says he couldn't get our conversation out of his head. Something had not sat right with him. He knew that his treasure box was never near the Baileys'. He assumed that any number of the pranksters in our family could have moved it. He also was confused about the notes to Jackson that I told him about.

For that reason, he decided to make some calls at his next land stop. He would never be able to explain exactly why.

The first was to the number I had given him for Chandler from the first day I met him when we exchanged contacts. He got Chandler on the first ring.

Taft discussed his visits to Culley, and Chandler bragged on everyone welcoming him so kindly. He told

Taft that he wouldn't be going to Culley this week 'cause he had caught a terrible head cold. This was apparent by his Donald Duck voice on the phone.

When Taft asked him about meeting up when he returned Chandler brushed it off. This seemed odd since he was there with the family attending service now.

He decided to move on to override the awkwardness.

You know your sister Kate was always so good to me. She understood who I was in the days when I was taboo. Did she ever marry?" Taft asked.

"No"

Realizing how impolite he sounded, he tried to explain in more detail.

"She is doing well and I don't get to see her as often as I would like."

Taft continued, "I have a guy that I may want to introduce to her. You and I can engineer the scenario like the old days, huh?"

"Taft, I said Kate isn't married, but she just ended her marriage. She is considering going back to him.

"She is just not in a very good place right now," Chandler said in a serious voice.

To this day, my uncle can't understand why, without hesitation, he wanted to call Kate.

He called his office and had them look up Kate Monnier from her hometown of Atlanta. The secretary did this within minutes. Her name was now Kate Monnier Martin.

He dialed the number he was given and got her voice mail. He left a message and went about the island to do some sightseeing.

He was excited about making contact with Kate. He remembered her as an artsy hippy sort of girl in college. Her apartment always had a pungent smell of incense. There was always a bandana on her head and never a stitch of make-up on her face.

Finally, about an hour later, Kate returned his call. They spoke for a few minutes about pleasantries.

Then, Taft explained that he had spoken with Chandler and knew about her recent divorce. He told her that he knew she was still somewhat undecided about getting back together with him.

There was silence on the line.

"I hope I'm not overstepping my boundaries," he said, embarrassed about bringing it up.

"No, not at all," Kate explained. "I am divorced, but not even remotely considering going back to him. I can't believe Chandler, of all people, would suggest that to you," she said curiously.

"Well, Chandler is surprising all of us these days," Taft explained.

"Why, he has been driving into Culley for Baptist service for the last two weeks," he continued.

Again, there was silence on the other end of the line. Taft could feel her pulling back and thinking about the conversation way too long.

"Taft, there is something terribly wrong here," she said in a frightened voice.

"What?" he asked, wondering if they just had a bad connection.

"Chandler is married and has been living in California for five years," she explained. "He is Catholic and, pardon me for saying so, would never attend a Baptist service," she continued.

"Kate, I just talked with him not two hours ago," Taft explained.

"I called his cell," Taft said and began reading the numbers off to Kate.

"Taft, that isn't Chandler's cell number," she said.

Then she read him the actual cell number that she knew belonged to her brother.

Uncle Taft quickly got off the phone with Kate, promising to call her back soon.

He dialed the cell number that Kate gave him. Instantly, a cheerful Chandler answered.

This was the voice of Chandler Monnier that my uncle had known. The second Taft heard it, he knew. That old familiar tone was there. He began explaining the details of the past few hours and all of the confusion.

Chandler had never been to Culley Cove in his life, and he gave Taft all of his contact information.

"Oh, Chandler, I think I know what this is all about," Uncle Taft said.

"I am prosecuting a case about a man who didn't follow protocol for his company dumping waste products," he explained.

"I figure the defense team has hired some nut job to go to Culley to snoop out more information about my great uncle mapping out a sewage fertilizer from his outhouse years ago," he explained. "Their team knew I was on a cruise and I'll bet they researched me and found you somewhere in my history during college,"

"Does it get that nasty, Taft?" Chandler asked.

"Oh, it gets lots worse than that," Taft said with a sigh.

As he hung up, his mind was swimming with anger. *I can't believe those defense attorneys. They will stop at nothing.*

He thought, *Lord there is no tellin' what Gammy has shared with the guy posing as Chandler by now.*

Taft quickly dialed Caroline's cell, but got voice mail. He decided it would be best for him to return and see what was going on rather than to upset everybody. If Gammy thought that the defense team was snooping on the Churchills' personal business, she would have Skeeter hang him from a tree, he thought.

Chapter 27

POOR MRS. MARSHALL
2001

Gammy picked me up at nine thirty for our drive into the city the next morning. She was on fire with plans to meet up with Mrs. Marshall.

On our way there, my cell phone rang and it was Osbourne's assistant from his office. He apologized for the short notice and regretted to tell us that Mrs. Marshall had suffered a heart attack and passed away during the night.

Gammy pulled over on the side of the road. She started humming "Amazing Grace" and then grabbed my hand and we had a prayer for Mrs. Marshall.

Then Gammy thought for a moment before banging on her steering wheel.

"Something is fighten' us, granddaughter! Don't you feel it?" she screamed.

"Yes, I do," I agreed.

"What is it you always say, Gammy? We have work to do," I reminded her.

I dialed Osbourne on my cell phone.

He seemed stunned himself. He had been over to make sure it was natural causes and not a result of our recent investigating.

"She went peacefully," he said. "She was sitting in her chair, looking at old photos, and just went into cardiac arrest," he summarized.

Gammy and I invited Osbourne to meet us for lunch in town since we were already there. He agreed more out of obligation to us than anything else.

None of us realized that this day was so similar to the last day of Jackson's life. Sinister plans were in motion and we didn't recognize them.

As we met with Osbourne, Gammy enjoyed explaining her feelings on the Churchills burying Jackson's murder under the rug. She said that she never approved, but it was for the good of the order.

Gammy's rant seemed to amuse Osbourne. She asked more questions about the necklaces. Gammy brought her little notebook to write down details she thought she might forget. Osbourne would look over and wink at me as she was writing.

"You know," Gammy said, "I know that whoever that SOB was, he had to have come in on one of the boats our marina sent from the repair shop. That is the only way he could get across the bridge to Culley proper unnoticed.

Now, Buckley, my husband, disagrees with me on the point. I think he is hung up on it being his fault if it was the way I am sayin'," she continued.

"Funny you say that, Mavis. We always suspected that too," Osbourne agreed.

"Once he got to Culley, he would have had to know his way around pretty well to go unseen, right?" he continued.

"Yes, sir!" Gammy shouted just a wee bit too loudly.

"So where would a person hide in a boat in those days?" he asked.

"Oh, lots of 'em had cabins in 'em. Yeah most of 'um were small, but a man could fit in 'em. Sure," Gammy concluded.

"Now my sons checked every one of them boats at the time. They never saw one single sign of anybody in the boats, but I just know it. I do," Gammy said, taking another slurp of her coffee.

We said our good-byes, and then Gammy and I left for Culley.

* * *

He peeked from behind the blinds of his courthouse office. He was surprised that the Churchills were finally getting serious about investigating after all of those years. Filled with rage, he wanted to act now. If he did, he knew he would be caught. He thought to himself that waiting would make it even more shocking.

Chapter 28

HE WATCHES FROM THE SAWGRASS
2001

Gammy and I pulled into town just in time to get ready for Wednesday service. Wit was already dressed when I entered our house.

Cleeve was hurrying me along so we wouldn't be late. He asked what Gammy and I were doing, and I explained having lunch and girl time together. It seemed logical, but Cleeve knew Gammy and I would just as well have done that outside on the dock or a porch. He just looked at me as if to give me his call on the BS.

* * *

As Pastor Caldwell stood, giving his sermon on forgiveness, he pointed to my mama.

"Now right over there we have a perfect example of a woman who brought forgiveness to her family. Sugar Churchill didn't want to let anger take over her world in the eyes of evil. She stood right up to that angry soul with goodness and *forgiveness*," he said.

Gammy and I shared glances, knowing that Mama hadn't forgiven; she had never even accepted, God bless her.

Pastor Caldwell chanted, "Matthew 5:44, *But I say to you, love your enemies and pray for those who persecute you.*"

"*Amen!*" Pee-Paw cheered, followed by Daddy.

Pastor Caldwell then shouted, "*Amen, Sister Sugar Churchill!*" While he was chanting, he pointed to my mama sitting in the second row.

Pastor went on with another tirade.

"Matthew 18:21–35," Pastor yelled. "*Then Peter came and said to Him, Lord, how often shall my brother sin against me and I forgive him? Up to seven times? Jesus said to him, I do not say to you, up to seven times, but up to seventy times seven.*"

Uncle Skeeter cheered, "*Amen!*" followed by Pee-Paw and then Daddy.

Then Pastor Caldwell again yelled, "*Amen, Sister Sugar Churchill!*"

This time he had walked down to where she was sitting. He asked Mama to stand. As she stood, he clapped for her.

"Aaah, strength!" he yelled, wiping sweat from his brow with his handkerchief.

At this, the congregation was getting so excited; the old men adjusted their hearing aids, which were now in song during each silent moment.

This night seemed like every other Wednesday service inside. I looked around for Chandler as I noticed Nita was wearing a new dress. *Maybe he had decided that we were too far out there for him,* I thought. Taft sure did like him, and for that reason alone, I needed to call him and invite him to come back.

* * *

Lurking outside the Culley Cove Baptist Church, he was waiting for the perfect moment. He listened to the singing of hymns. He was laughing at goodness, which he interpreted as stupidity.

He began to sing in his demented voice in the saw grass.

I can sing, Daddy.
I can sing.
I could have been famous in a rock band, Daddy.
You couldn't believe.
Believe in yourself and let those you love believe too.
Why couldn't you, Daddy?
Why couldn't you?
I showed you, Daddy

I showed you, didn't I?
I took you out, Daddy, didn't I?

He sang his dark words, believing that murdering his own father had somehow made him superior.

Chapter 29

TONIGHT IS THE NIGHT
2001

Taft had managed to catch a pricy flight into Miami. He knew he would have to wait at the airports until he could catch flights into Tallahassee, which wasn't always easy to do. Then he would still have to rent a car for a two-hour drive into Culley.

You see, at this point, Uncle Taft was still convinced that this imposter was trying to get dirt on him about a case he was prosecuting. Poor Taft had figured this was a big blowhole about pollution in North Florida. Also, whoever was pretending to be Chandler clearly said he wouldn't be at service tonight. Taft planned to go and just check everything out until he found a way to have an unexpected word with the imposter.

Wit had fixed the best peach cobbler that night for dessert. He had made it at Mama and Daddy's since we were having supper there. We were all bragging on his culinary gifts when the phone rang. Mama answered it, and it was obvious it was Taft.

"Oh, yeah, Taft. She is right here having some of the best peach cobbler you can imagine," Mama said, glancing at me while licking ice cream off her fingers.

I grabbed the phone, and Taft asked me to find a private place to talk. I walked out onto the back porch and plopped down on the bench swing.

"What on God's green earth, Uncle Taft?" I asked, starting to swing slightly.

"Girl, that guy there is not Chandler," Taft said.

"Taft, are you high?" I asked.

"Caroline, seriously, he is from the defense team in Orlando. I think they are trying to get information about Culley being polluted years ago by a Churchill," he continued.

"For Lord's sake, don't say a word to anybody. Gammy will have him tarred and feathered by morning." He laughed.

He explained that he had spoken with the real Chandler Monnier. I had a mind's image of Nita's disappointed face as the lyrics of "Another One Bites the Dust" played in my head.

"You know this really pisses me off, Taft! The nerve," I said

"Promise me you won't get all fired up and do anything, OK?" Taft asked.

"Well, what are we gonna do?" I asked.

"I won't have him coming up here sucking up to my gammy!" I raised my voice.

"I know. Just do your best for the night to keep the conversation or any phone calls to him off the table," Uncle Taft said.

"I need your help on this one, sweetie, OK?" he asked. "Dorothy ain't in Kansas no more," he said with a smile in his voice.

"OK Uncle Taft," I said. "But I don't like it one bit!" I pouted.

"I know, darlin'. I know," he said. "Just try to keep your radar out on all of it and don't let the universes collide until I can get down there. I am about to fly into Tallahassee, and then I will drive into Culley tonight. It will be a surprise. Can I come straight to your house so Gammy and Pee-Paw don't shoot me tonight thinkin' I am breaking in?" he asked.

"I'll have the linens on the guest bed, sweet Uncle," I said. "You still have your key?" I asked.

"Yes, ma'am," he said.

After the call, I retreated to the kitchen for a second helping of cobbler and ice cream. Our family was laughing hysterically as Wit was telling funny stories.

Mama and Daddy's old dog Rufus was underneath the table. I was slipping him some pieces of leftover chicken from my dirty plate. Mama saw me and just shook her head as if I would never grow up.

That evening, in many ways, was parallel to the last morning we had with Jackson. Don't get me wrong, because none of us had any notion of that then, but looking back, we do. In fact, we were eating and laughing like we did that morning. We had sat at this same table in this same room in 1978. We had the same sadistic soul lurking and watching our routines and our relationships.

As we cleaned the dishes, Mama and I talked about Wit's grades. She went on and on about how smart he was and how everyone was jealous of him.

"He is so much like your brother, Caroline," she said.

I looked over at her. There were no words. Years of defeat came over me. This game was part of her survival.

I couldn't talk about Jackson without mentioning the reality so it was better not to talk about him with Mama. I simply leaned over the sink and planted a kiss on her cheek. It was like the morning when I was leaving for the party. I couldn't tell her what our plans really were that night. I had to tell her what she needed to hear. We wanted to sneak out, but in light of what happened, I am now glad we all chickened out.

After the dishes were done, we all sat on the back porch and talked for a long while. Wit had started telling us stories again; it was so similar to the way Jackson used to. He was very animated, and I couldn't help but notice Mama's laughing tears. Boy, we hadn't seen those much in the past years. My Wit lit her up in a way that I don't think even she could explain.

Daddy started teasing Mama, and she would reprimand him in fun. Cleeve was offering some insight on some new boat ideas he had for the Marina when Rufus started barking.

"Rufus!" Daddy shouted, "*get on!*"

* * *

Behind the wire grass, he was kneeling down, watching Titus Churchill yell at Rufus for his warning.

In his small voice he said, "Yeah, Rufus...get on! Don't warn the fools."

He then just sat in wait for his plans to unravel in the dark of night.

Chapter 30

IMPATIENCE IS NOT BECOMING
2001

Cleeve and I tucked Wit into bed, and then walked back into the living room to watch TV together. It was then I told him about my call from Uncle Taft. He was in disbelief over Chandler being such a liar.

"You Churchills are like a good television drama." Cleeve laughed.

"So Chandler is a guy hired by an attorney to find out about an old uncle's outhouse setup? Boy, that Uncle Fiddler of yours caused more trouble with his toilet," Cleeve said as he doubled over laughing.

"Wait!" I explained. "Remember, it really isn't Chandler." I giggled.

"So who is it?" Cleeve asked, still laughing while crossing his eyes at me.

"A defense attorney or someone a defense attorney sent, I think," I said before we both burst back into giggles.

"So who is Chandler?" Cleeve asked again.

We were teasing each other about the confusion.

"Poor Nita," I said, glancing back at the television.

"I would say poor whoever this Chandler guy is or the one pretending to be Chandler after Gammy gets hold of him," Cleeve said, laughing just thinking of it.

We went to bed around ten thirty that evening. I had fallen into a deep sleep that night. I didn't awake until around two o'clock. It was then I looked over at Cleeve and he was sound asleep. I put on my robe and headed outside for the dock. As I approached the wood, I noticed that Tripod wasn't with me. I looked around and even softly called his name.

Tripod was nowhere to be found outside. I walked back into the house to make sure I hadn't shut him in. The dog door was opened, so I assumed he was where he wanted to be. *Old crazy fool dog*, I thought.

I shrugged it off with images of the old dog digging and exploring more lately. I missed him, but felt happy for him that he was finding his confidence in his surroundings. When we found him, he was a bag of bones. He was scared of his own shadow for weeks until he built up trust in us. Old Tripod and I had found our strength together these last few months.

* * *

"That's it, Caroline," he said to himself in his wicked high-pitched voice. He was peeking from behind the pines and marsh grass.

"I wouldn't hurt your dog," he said out loud to himself. *"I just incapacitated him for a while with some sleeping medicine,"* he continued. *"My own Daddy used to do that to me when he wanted me to shut up."*

I can be mean, he thought, *but I am not cruel.*

He believed that he was a good person in his own right. He had a mission that drove him to do work for others. He was protecting the rights of all who had their dreams taken away by family.

I would never harm an animal. No, only people, Caroline Churchill Burton.

He was silent at first and then fell back into his baby-light voice. "Walk out to your old dock that your pee-paw made for you and open your silly wooden box," he whispered like a broken doll.

"Your brother stopped Taft from starting our band. I needed that band!" he chirped to himself wiping sweat off his forehead with his sleeve.

He was getting angrier as his heart raced in the dead of night.

His thoughts were fast and robotic.

Now he stopped and barely inhaled. He watched as Caroline used her flashlight to unlock her special box.

He knew that she would find some surprises once she opened it. *This will be fun to watch,* he thought with excitement.

Chapter 31

PEACE ON THE DOCK WILL NOT COME TONIGHT
2001

I hesitated to open my box. Instead, I looked out over the water, placing it down beside me. I thought about Taft and how, in his own way, he had tried to be a brother to me. I really never gave him enough credit for that.

My mind then swam to Mrs. Marshall. The poor lady had died alone, not knowing what really happened. At least she tried. She faced it.

* * *

Pick up the box and open it, Caroline, he thought. He was waiting impatiently.

* * *

Then I reached down for my box and opened it. I held my light down onto the box to show exactly what was in it.

I noticed immediately there were pictures and envelopes in my box that didn't belong there. A sharp chill ran down my spine. I knew someone had been in my box. I looked up and surveyed my surroundings. I appeared to be alone. Only Wit knew where the key and box were.

The first photo was of Taft and Chandler. It was the Chandler that had been pretending to be Chandler, not the real one.

On the back of the photo was written "Max and Taft, 1978."

"Max," I said out loud, remembering Mrs. Marshall's story from several days before.

Max was the band member who was so angry with her son, Danny. Ted had gotten on the phone with Max and asked him to ease up on his brother.

My hands were shaking so badly I could barely manage digging in the box. There were several envelopes that had been folded into small pieces.

As I opened the first one, I pulled out the small photo inside it. It was a picture of Jackson and Chandler. My brain switched gears. No, not Chandler. Max!

I turned the photo over and saw the small writing. "Max and Jackson."

I stared at it in confusion for a moment. My eyes went over it as I noticed Jackson's red shirt and his hair. It was the day he went missing. I looked around and saw that it was taken at the Bailey house.

I'm gonna tell you right now that at that moment, I thought my heart would beat right out of my chest. Tears began waterfalling down my cheeks, but I couldn't even feel them.

I tore through the next envelope and there was a picture of Mrs. Marshall. She was in her living room on the same sofa as the other day. She was holding a photo book.

The next envelope had a picture of Mrs. Marshall holding pictures in her lap. She appeared to be unconscious.

Then I noticed the blue coloration on her lips. Jesus, she was dead! *Lord in heaven, who is playin' with my head? This is a photo of Mrs. Marshall dead as a doornail. It must have been taken just this morning,* I thought.

Finally, the last envelope said *Important* on the outside. I slowly opened it as my hands trembled uncontrollably. I pulled out the photo. It was familiar. It was a picture of a body with a red shirt on the rock at the Baileys'. It was Jackson. He was dead. This was the image that I had only imagined for most of my life.

My cry was primal as my mother's had been the day she found out Jackson was gone. The same as her cry in the church at the service. My heart couldn't possibly hurt any more than it did already. I suddenly felt numb. It was then that I heard a creak behind me on the dock.

* * *

"Hello, Caroline Churchill Burton," Max Gridley said in a low toying voice.

"I suppose by now you realize I am not Chandler Monnier," he continued.

"You son of a bitch!" I screamed. I didn't even think of it before running toward him and pushing him as hard as I could. His strength surprised me as he grabbed my arm tightly. The pain shot through my body. He force walked me to the end of the dock. I struggled and then he leaned down and whispered in my ear.

"You saw the photos. You know what I am capable of doing?" Don't make me go inside the house and send your little Wit up to meet his Uncle Jackson! Isn't Wit about the age you were when Jackson was murdered?"

"NO!" I cried.

He was laughing at me.

"Oh, you Churchills are funny people. I will give you that," he said, sounding like a mouse.

"As wonderful as you all claim to be with your sweet tea and yes, ma'ams, you don't let your own family be true to themselves, do you!"

All I could think was that I hoped Cleeve would wake up and remember how to use that old gun in the closet. God love him. He wasn't raised like us in the sticks, using guns all of the time.

Chapter 32

MY BOOGEYMAN
2001

"You know it was really so easy, Caroline," he said as he pulled the loose rope off his wrist, pushing me to the ground. He straddled me while reinforcing his threat to Wit. Then he moved down to my legs and started tying the rope around my knees.

"What are you doing?" I asked.

"I am tying your knees together. Now, you can still swim if you want to," he said, cackling.

"What?" I asked completely confused.

Was he challenging me? I thought as my mind spun in circles.

"I waited at the café right there where your daddy and pee-paw worked that day," he continued, *enjoying making me listen.*

"I walked around pretending to be fascinated with the old boats. Your family just had receipts right there in each boat that had been serviced. They told exactly when boats were to be delivered back across to Culley Cove," he continued.

"You know that was really a dumb way of doing business, Caroline? He said, smiling.

"You should talk to them about that since I see they are still doing it that way today." He laughed.

"Oh, that's right. If you can't swim with your knees bound you won't be able to tell them anything," he said as he roared with laughter.

"What are you going to do, Max?" I asked.

He laughed again, clearly enjoying the control way too much.

"Oh, you already got my name, huh? You figured out that I'm not sweet Chandler Monnier from college. OOOOh, that was so good," he said half laughing. Very well done, Caroline Churchill Burton," he teased.

"Why don't you jump, Caroline?" he continued.

"You have tied my knees together!" I whispered harshly.

"You could still swim but it wouldn't be easy," he said, hopeful I would try.

Now he cocked his head like a bird and laughed.

"Old Mrs. Marshall told you way too much, didn't she? I had to shut that old bird up." He scowled, gesturing his eyes to the pictures.

"She had a different reaction to the pictures," he continued. "She had a heart attack. You cried." He smiled.

"There is another picture in there that you have missed," he said looking at my box.

My beautiful box Jackson had given me. The treasure I got on my last normal morning.

I dug down and pulled out the last of the mysterious envelopes and in it was a photo of Osbourne. He was alive, but it was taken early that day when Gammy and I had lunch with him.

"Now, I am saving him for last because I want to show him a picture of you with your special necklace, sweet Caroline," he said, now laughing.

"How did you know how to get into my box?" I asked, holding back tears.

"That is one of the greatest parts of all," Max Gridley said. "Your son, Wit, told me. Yes, he betrayed your trust, didn't he? You know your son that looks so much like Jackson?"

"You are an evil person! May God have mercy on your mean-assed soul!" I cried to him looking up toward heaven beyond the moon.

After all of these years, the boogeyman in my dreams had come to life. This was the face of the monster in my dreams. It was not as I had expected. The face was attractive and normal. His ability to transform into whatever he needed to be had worked on us. I hated that fact as my brain was wrapping around the understanding of it all. How could we have allowed him into our circle in Culley? He had been eating and talking with us. He had worshipped with us in our church.

Chapter 33

THE LONG DRIVE TO
CULLEY COVE
2001

Taft had managed to get into Tallahassee and rent a car that night. He was on his way into Culley as I was fighting for my life on my dock.

As he drove east on Interstate 10, he thought of his college days.

Taft remembers that flying into Tallahassee had him thinking back on his college band days. He wondered what that crazy Max had ever made of himself. He would need to ask Chandler if he knew.

Max had made him face some realities about himself. For that, no one could deny. Max had come from a wealthy family and never seemed quite right. He had kept on to them about the band in an obsessive kind of way. He was the real reason none of them wanted to continue it. Max would have them practice over and over until they were sick of it. The perfection was too intense for the other members. Then he seemed to be obsessed with knowing every detail of Taft's life.

At one point, the entire band quit, and Max went out and bought each of them brand-new top-of-the-line instruments as an apology. They played a bit longer, and Max decided that he wanted it to be just him and Taft playing together. They would do the guitar and singing together and just hire out a drummer.

Max wouldn't take no for an answer. He followed Taft around and one time even tried to ask if Taft found him attractive. Taft knew he had to get away from him before he was identified for his own orientation.

He had talked to Jackson about it at camp that summer. Jackson and Taft sat outside of the tents after hours talking. Taft had been trying to come to terms with his sexual identity. Many of his unsettled feelings had been brought to light by his friend in the band. He wanted to be a part of the band. He was a good musician, but the Churchills wanted a lawyer in the family. Jackson had told him that something was wrong with Max. He wasn't normal.

Taft was driving and thinking back on all of it. He remembered the letter to Max. It had just been a band. It never had connected Taft's brain to Jackson or Culley. The situations were so disconnected.

As he began to accelerate on the interstate, he started reconnecting the dots with the defense attorneys. Surely, that is what this is about, he thought, sipping his frappuccino.

Just then, his cell phone rang.

"Hello, Taft," Max said into the phone."

"Who is this?"

"This is Max Gridley. Surely you remember me. I made you face your truth! You betrayed me!"

Taft was silent.

"I have someone special here with me. Your sweet niece Caroline is standing right here with me."

"What!"

"This is the deal, Taft old boy," he continued. "If you don't hang up with me I won't kill her. Right now anyway. Better yet, I could go inside and surprise the little one," he said, winking his right eye at me. "If you do and I know you are trying to call somebody else, you can find one or both of them on a huge rock by the Baileys'. You know that rock, right, Taft? You know where Jackson was found lifeless?"

"Why! Why did you kill Jackson?" Taft was yelling into the phone uncontrollably.

"Because I watched and listened to the two of you at the camp. It made me sick."

"You weren't at the camp that summer!"

"I wasn't teaching or a student but I was there."

"Where?"

"In the woods."

"Doing what?"

"Watching and listening to you and Jackson talking about how weird I am."

"Why?"

"I wanted to see if you were going to betray me like all the others.

"What?"

"Jackson and I were arguing about it. At that time I wasn't sure what I was going to do."

"No, I saw the way you absorbed everything Jackson said. He had convinced you that I was insane. He had to go!"

There it was. The reason that my brother died was answered. The reason that my life had been altered was answered. The reason that my entire family had lived in a shell was answered. It was all because a crazy person had a crush on my gay uncle. My brother knew Max was insane and talked Uncle Taft into ending the relationship. His gift of goodness had been the same element that ended his life.

Chapter 34

WHO IS MAX?
2001

Max Gridley and I stood on my dock, staring at each other in the moonlight. I was wearing my coffee cup print robe and he was in a black body suit. The only part of him that could be seen was his head.

"Taft!" I screamed.

"Caroline, I'm here," Taft said almost in tears.

"He and I are on the dock," I explained so that he knew how to find me if it was possible.

"He can't call anybody, Caroline, and poor Cleeve can't wake up 'cause I put sleeping juice on his toothbrush while you were over at your parents' house." He grinned. "I am superior, Caroline," he said.

I could hear Taft pleading with Max on the phone.

"Now, Taft, I need you and your niece to listen to my story," Gridley said.

Your niece has taken it upon herself to finally take an interest in reality. I want to give it to her and you first hand.

"If you stop listening, Taft old boy, you can come to the rock. Of course, you will be too late," he continued with the confidence of a news anchor's voice.

"I recognize you, don't I, Max?" I asked, more certain of it that ever.

"Well, I don't know, Caroline Churchill Burton. Do you?" he asked smugly.

My mind flashed back to the first time I met Max behind the church. That feeling that I had as if I had known him before. He had acted so shocked that we didn't think he was important. This was the missing piece my mind couldn't find that day.

Suddenly, just like Doc Chapman had told me, I explored my memory. I saw it. I remembered more than I had the day after Jackson left.

"You were at the Baileys' house when Jackson and I walked by, I continued. "You walked out and asked him when Taft was coming in. You were so casual, and he trusted you," I said, holding back tears.

"You used Uncle Taft's name then just like you did now with all of us," I said. "You claimed to be his friend!"

"I cannot confirm or deny that, Caroline Churchill Burton," Max said almost in a song.

"You said you were supposed to wait for Taft at the Baileys' house. You told Jackson that Taft wanted him to come back too and ya'll may go fishing later together." I could see them standing there talking in my mind so perfectly. This memory had been lost in time for so long.

I continued, "The bird dogs were wailing and Jackson said he should really go on and feed them. Then Jackson looked at me and..." I started crying.

"Finish, Caroline," Max looked at me cruelly as he watched my memory connect its pieces.

"Jackson looked at you, and you pouted about going to your stupid party, right?" Max said.

"Do you blame yourself for that, Caroline?" he asked.

"Your sweet brother told you that he would take you to the party and come back to meet me. He was such a selfless guy, wasn't he?

"I waited right there for him too, Caroline. He was back in fifteen minutes or so. He was a dutiful soldier. A true Churchill," he joked.

"When he got back I had Taft's box with me. Oh, did that make your Jackson mad," Max said.

"He asked how I got it and I told him that Taft told us college boys about the secret boxes you kept hidden. He had told us where his was, never dreaming one of us would ever care enough to get to Culley and hunt for it," he sang in his crazed voice.

Now, Taft was yelling into the phone for him to stop. My mind raced to Taft and all of his fancy phones. He may be able to pull something off. If he did, it would have to be lightning fast or Max would catch it.

Then my attention went back to the insane man on my dock.

"Oh, you were right, Taft," Max said. "Your Culley folks are so very friendly.

"I waited at that café," he said. "When I saw everyone out talking at the end of the day, that was when I made my move," he explained.

"I went to the boat I had already selected. I got in the cabin of it and closed the doors. Those men were clueless. They were talking right there beside me while I was setting up myself as a castaway," he continued.

"Good old Uncle Skeeter hooked the boat to his trailer and drove me across the bridge," he explained.

"He pulled me right up to the Churchill Marina, unhooked the trailer, and headed to his house. He was whistling 'Shadow Dancing' by Andy Gibb. I remember 'cause I liked that song too," he added with a giggle.

Max was clearly crazy as a loon. His voice was child-like and his face in a trance.

"The owner of the boat was to pick it up the next morning. It said so right there on the ticket." Max laughed.

Then he whispered, "I just lay there in that cabin for hours. Hell, I fell asleep for a long time. That is how certain I was that I was among the stupid," he sneered. "My dad would have been so proud of my superior thinking.

"Around four in the morning, I got out of the boat and used my flashlight to check my maps," he explained. "I already had everything memorized. I walked over to the old fishing docks where Taft's box was. I used some of the old equipment there and dug it up. I tell you, it couldn't have played smoother than if it was directed for a movie," he bragged.

"Then, I took the letter that Taft had left for me, ending my dream," he continued. "The same note that disallowed me to be true to myself. I placed it in his box," he said with his voice rising.

"Later, I took the letter Taft had written to your sweet Jackson," he explained. "I placed it in the box too. You see, I found it the day before Taft was going to give it to him.

"Old Taft was bragging to your brother about his wisdom for telling him to release me," Max continued. "It was a sickening letter! Sickening!" he said, whimpering.

"I knew it would be there with Jackson's body," he explained. "I hoped it would be found, which is why I buried it so lightly and close to Jackson's body. I never dreamed it would take you slow movers decades and even then a three legged dog would be the founder."

Chapter 35

GAMMY ALWAYS TOLD ME TO MARK MY TERRITORY
2001

There is one thing about us folks who grow up spending a lot of time outside. You trust your instincts and know your territory. I knew my yard and the sights and sounds of it like the back of my hand. I had spent enough time on my dock to know its creaks and movements with the water and wind. I never knew I would need that knowledge, but that night I was sure as hell glad I had it.

It's for that reason that I just happened to notice a little movement in the trees. I didn't know who or what it was. I put together that if Taft had managed to make a call during this fool's long-winded account of his craziness that the timing would be about right for help.

I scooted over as best I could with my knees tied. I knew I looked awkward but figured Max would enjoy the control he had over me. I managed to sit down on the bench facing the water, hoping this insane man would sit beside me. If he did, he would be turned away from the entry of the dock if help should come. As I sat, I gracefully looked up at the moon. I intentionally did so as if it was just for comfort.

This angered him, but he was curious.

"Caroline, am I boring you?"

"No, but your story is upsetting and these ropes are hurting me. I feel light-headed," I explained.

"I need to sit and I want to look at the moon," I continued. "You of all people believe in us being true to ourselves. That is what my body is telling me to do now, Max,"

He sat beside me and looked at the moon briefly. It was clear that he didn't find the same peacefulness. Looking at him, I wondered if he had ever loved anyone. Was he capable? Were people born this way or did their life experiences shaped it?

Now we were both sitting with our backs to the entry of the dock. This was all that I needed to focus on for now.

I knew who he was now. I could make predictions about his actions. There were no guarantees because he was so obviously disturbed. I knew that I could try to play to his ego. He would have never expected me to get help way out on the dock. I suppose Max felt so superior that he never dreamed we could ruin his plans.

"Taft, you better still be on that phone!" he shouted into the phone, while gazing at the water.

"I wouldn't go anywhere if I thought you might hurt my niece," he said.

"Well now, Caroline, if you are quite comfortable and Taft is on the line, may I continue?" he said in an arrogant tone.

"Jackson did as he said he would and came back. He almost blew the whole plan, though. He mentioned taking another boy fishing with us. He said the kid was weird, but we should ask him," he said.

"Ustus!" I said.

"Whatever! He shouted at me. "It's my turn! Don't interrupt me! It's rude! Very rude!" Max yelled.

He had realized I wasn't going to try to swim for his amusement. He squatted down and began tying my ankles together as he spoke.

"Jackson had told the boy he would find out if it was OK for him to join and would go back and let him know. Well, your brother never made it back to let the weird boy know," Max said.

"That's when I confronted Jackson about letting his uncle be true to himself," Max continued, "Your Jackson thought he was superior to me. I could see it in his eyes. His expression was telling me that he had no respect for me."

Max then leaned forward and ran his fingers through his hair. He was getting agitated, but I wasn't sure why.

After a while, he started again. "Your Jackson actually asked me if we could sit down and talk it over! Can you believe that? This kid was younger than me and didn't have my pedigree or education. The idea of him challenging me and trying to predict my behavior!" Max was spitting now as he spoke.

"Then your silly Jackson motioned for me to follow him and told me that he and Taft had this special fishing hole over by the rock. He was excited to show it off. Can you believe how mean that was? I was no longer even allowed to be friends with Taft and this kid is showing me where he and Taft like to fish. He was leaving me out, but showing me what they liked to do," Max said, breathing heavily now.

Max sat still, just thinking for a moment. I tried not to even consider what might be going through that crazed brain. It would be too scary for me right then.

Finally, he continued, "We sat down on that huge rock. Then, your brother started talking. Your Jackson told me, 'In the Churchill family we support each other. We try to do what is right for our family. I didn't mean any harm, but I think you are bad for my Uncle Taft.'

"Jackson then went on to tell me, 'My uncle knows where my treasure box is and he has never touched it.' As your Jackson said this, he glanced down over there in those trees," Max said, gesturing his hands. "I caught it and knew that his box was there."

Then Max moved right down into my face. I could smell his rancid breath.

"You never could find it and I came in and discovered it in one day!" he squealed.

"God in heaven what is wrong with you?" I said before even knowing the words had left the station of my mouth.

"Wrong with me? Wrong with me?" he screamed blowing spit in all directions.

He stopped himself, wiping his face with his sleeve. Then he grabbed my arm tightly.

"Listen carefully, Caroline," Max Gridley said, barely opening his mouth to talk. "I want you and Taft to hear this part. I want to watch your face as you hear it," he taunted.

"Look at me!" he shouted as he placed the necklace around my neck as he had done with Jackson. I stared at the guitar stings wrapped in wire. Now I knew he planned to kill me for sure. I was to be found with this foolish necklace around my neck. Mrs. Marshall's sweet face danced in my mind.

Then he continued speaking in his calm voice, "I took my knife and I stabbed your Jackson as many times as I could," Max said.

His words pierced my heart in a way that physically took my breath, but I refused to let Gridley see it. He wouldn't enjoy hurting our family anymore. If for only this moment, if I could not show the emotion, I would feel stronger for it.

He examined my face for any sadness, but I refused to give him that satisfaction. I just forced a solid look.

Max then went on with evil intent.

"He never said anything. He just stared until he couldn't anymore. Then I took a rock from over there underneath the cypress tree. I crushed his head with it."

Max said this as if he were asking me about the weather.

"It was so easy," he continued. "Then I made sure everything inside had been done as Taft had mentioned so many times. He told us all about the Baileys and how he used their house to hang out while they were away," Max explained.

"Your brother was gone. I thought Taft could be free. You hear this, Taft?" he shouted into the phone.

"I'm here," Taft said as if he had no air left.

"That's what I thought, Taft," Gridley ranted, "that you would be free.

"No, Taft, you changed completely after that. We never saw you. Then you just transferred to another school. After all I did for you, this is what you gave back?" he said, now crying like a small child.

Then, Max grabbed me and took me right to the edge of my dock. He leaned me over the water. I could hear the crashing of the incoming tide underneath us. The water I loved so much was threatening me.

"You are a demon on this earth!" I said holding back my tears. I would not cry. He wouldn't get that pleasure from me.

"Taft, are you listening?" he asked.

"Yes," he answered. "I'm here."

I could tell by my uncle's voice that he was frightened. I knew what he would like to say to this insane man who was controlling us. I also knew as Taft did that we had to tread lightly.

I had to hope that Taft had made it and was walking up to help me. I couldn't look back or Max would follow my gaze.

"Caroline...silly, scared girl who jumps from her dock to face her own fears because she can't do it every day of her life." He laughed.

"I want Taft to hear you plunge from your dock now," Max yelled. *"Gammy will not laugh at this jump when she finds you tied up soaked in salt water."* He cackled like an old witch.

Then he continued, "I will have you bound so you cannot swim to the shore tonight. Let us all hear how fearless you are as you fall into the water. Fight your fears! Fight me!" he whispered loudly.

"Maybe you can just do as your pathetic mother does and pretend. I know. Let's just tell ourselves that the water isn't there or you can breathe underneath it. That will make it all better, right?" He tilted his head back to give a gravelled cackle.

"Don't you see, Caroline Churchill Burton? Even now, if you shouldn't actually drown, which you will, you will always be afraid of your dock," *he* said as he squinted at me.

"The beauty of it is your own mother will likely tell you to just believe the dock doesn't exist." He roared as he started his knots in the ropes.

"The tide is coming in and no one will find you until low tide in the daylight hours. I will be long gone by then."

Max then put the phone down and started tying my wrists together. Taft was pleading with him on the phone, and we could hear it.

"Taft, you know you are pleading with me just as I pled with you to remain friends with me. We could have created songs that would have moved this world. You didn't care about my being true to myself. Guess what? I don't care about you now." He laughed, enjoying the retaliation.

As he was tying my wrists in anticipation of throwing me to my salty tomb right off my dock, he looked at me as if we were talking at dinner. How could I reason with insanity? There was no way to predict his actions.

In my own mind, I started praying to God in heaven to help guide this man to leave me alone. I then asked to help guide my family to help me. Finally, I prayed that if I died that Wit not be the one to find me.

When he finished obsessing over the knot in the rope around my wrists he said, "Now, I wonder how Gammy will handle this?"

He mocked Gammy's voice, *"Jackson and Caroline gone right here on her Churchill property."*

Then Max said, "What do you think now Gammy?"

Just then, Gammy yelled, "Why don't you ask me yourself, you dumb crazy ass?"

Well, you can imagine what all my gammy may have said, but it wouldn't be proper for me to write it.

Pee-Paw stood about ten yards back with his rifle positioned right on Gridley. He was wearing his little seersucker pajamas with a long robe over them.

Gammy Mavis Churchill held that gun as steady as a seasoned woodsman. She was still in her floral night-gown, which was budding out from the dark jacket she had over it.

She closed one eye, levelled her rifle down to Max Gridley's knee, and shot. As she fired, she said simply, "*Jackson!*"

I heard old Max scream in pain. I heard some of the wood fall from my dock into the water.

Hearing him hurt felt good to me. Maybe that makes me cruel, but, Lord, he deserved to feel pain.

Then, as she squinted again, aimed, and shot his other knee. As she fired, the second time she yelled, "*Caroline!*"

Max's screams were heard over the approaching sirens. My yard suddenly was illuminated like a disco ball as the patrol cars pulled in.

Finally, my gammy, Mavis Churchill, aimed that rifle at Max Gridley's privates. She smiled at old Gridley, who was pleading with her.

"*Are you pleading with me?*" she asked him, mocking his high-pitched voice.

She clicked her gun, ready for another fire, when we heard Osbourne yell from the dock entry, "OK, Mavis! We've got it."

She glanced up at Osbourne and said in a matter-of-fact voice, "I've got it too!" Then she shot.

Max Gridley's testicles went straight off the dock. They have never been recovered. Gammy says the bait-fish probably ate 'em.

As Osbourne and the others approached the dock, Gammy leaned over Max and whispered, "That's what Gammy would say, if you're still wonderin'!"

Chapter 36

MY BROTHER'S BOX
2001

The day after the testicular explosion off the dock, Nita and gammy organized a dinner at our house. I didn't cook because I was still too shaken up, but the church brought enough food for us to live underground for a year.

I was feeding an exhausted Tripod food under the table. The ordeal had confused his poor old brain to no end. I'm sure he had never been given sleeping medicine before. Gridley had put it inside a few bacon strips.

We were discussing the unbelievable events of the day before.

Osbourne had joined us that evening for dinner. He had spent the entire day with Gridley and a forensic psychologist.

Bless his heart; he was doing his best to explain everything Max had shared with him. So many aspects of our missing puzzle were finally coming together.

Osbourne was embarrassed that Max had been working right there in the courthouse and had become a coffee buddy with him. He was now explaining Gridley's confessions to us.

He told about Max stalking us as he concocted his evil plans. He was relieved to have put an end to the first case he had ever worked on as an assistant. Max pretended to have an interest in cold cases and had convinced Osbourne that he wanted to help out with them so that maybe one day he could work in that department.

His real name was Max Gridley Mason. He had conveniently left off the Mason part so that Osbourne wouldn't recognize him as the son of the widowed doctor that was murdered years before. Max had murdered his own father. Later, he called the house help, firing them by phone then mailing them checks from his father's account. He had managed to withdraw most of his daddy's money before sending the police over to discover the body. Max was pure evil.

Gammy slurped her coffee, leaned forward, and then asked, "Are you tellin' me he was just squattin' down in the saw grass watchin' and listenin' to us?"

"Yes, ma'am," Osbourne confirmed.

"Crazy fool!" Gammy snorted. "He come right up here and pretended to worship with us. I fixed the nut plates of food and all," Gammy continued, shaking her head.

"Well, I figure I was helpin' the crazy-assed sinner out," Gammy explained.

"He seemed so fond of hiding out in them bushes, singing with his high-pitched voice," she said. "Maybe now he will be full-time high pitch without any male parts." She laughed as we all joined in.

"Gammy!" Mama said, looking down.

"A psychopath often tries to find protection from being caught" Osbourne explained. "Typically, their strength is to conspire with law enforcement. He played me like a fiddle."

Gammy's mouth was wide open as she listened to Osbourne explain what he had learned about the Max and others like him.

"He's just crazy as hell!" Gammy said without thinking.

"Gammy!" Mama warned in a whisper as she glanced at Osbourne.

"His kind commonly invades circles of friends and family to develop relationships like he did with all of us. They don't have a conscience so there is no guilt. This helps them to hyper focus on their victims. They can suck you in like a black hole by observing, and manipulating situations to make way for their ambush." He explained as he reached for a napkin from Mama.

As Mama was serving coffee and dessert, Osbourne looked over at me and said, "Caroline, I believe this is for you." He handed me an old box.

The shark was right there on the top. I knew immediately that this was my brother's secret safety deposit box by the sea.

That was Max Gridley's only good deed. He disclosed the location of Jackson's box. I ran my fingers over the shark. I could see Jackson in my mind. He was so peaceful. The box I had only dreamed of finding so that Jackson could communicate with me one last time.

Then, I noticed that there was a lock on the old box. The keyhole looked so old. My heart was racing.

I jumped up and ran to get my box off the dock. From inside of it, I grabbed the old key I had found years before in Jackson's fishing jacket. I popped the box open. Inside were pictures of all of us. My favorite was the one of us as kids covered in mud, running around behind Gammy and Pee-Paw's.

Jackson had other things in there I took out in respect of his privacy. Had I found this box years before it would have explained so much to me about my uncle and my brother. Jackson had his own secrets about who he was and who he wanted to be. Those were his and I will not disclose them. I agreed with Mama about this one topic: personal business should stay personal. He wouldn't have minded me seeing them, but I knew how he would expect me to filter the contents.

I looked out at the moon and just felt peace. The first peace I had known since that morning in my cupcake room in 1978. It was as if Jackson was talking to me from heaven. He knew Max Gridley couldn't hurt us or anyone else.

I will always believe he was trying to help me find the answers. Gridley confessed to killing many others. If they got in his way, they became targets.

Jackson was just smiling at me in my mind. I smelled the box, but there was no Jackson smell. It had been outside way too long for that. This solidified the fact that it had indeed been a long time since he left. It was time for us to move forward. It was time for acceptance once and for all.

After I gained my composure, I took the box back to the family that evening. We all looked through it. There was laughter and tears as we combed through Jackson's last mystery.

Afterward, Gammy asked, "So what in the heck is the big blessed deal about burying secrets in a box and digging it back up? For Lord's sake, young'ins, just keep the secret in your head and nobody will ever get into it." She cackled, and we all smiled.

"It's just fun to have a tradition, Gammy," I explained.

"Lord, I reckon Buckley's gone have to go put me a deposit box by the sea together so I can go bury it. If the wrong person finds mine, I may not be past the statute of limitations on some of my secrets. Ya'll gone come and bail me out of the jailhouse?" She laughed.

We never knew that she was serious about wanting a special box like ours. I suppose the more Gammy thought about it, the more determined she was to do it. She did what she wanted and rarely had time to regret it.

Epilogue

GAMMY'S LEGACY

So here you have most of our Churchill story. As always in a good story, you save the best for last. I believe in this particular story, I do owe my gammy her special ending. She would expect that from me as a true Churchill.

We are proud small-town folks who try to live each day doing the best we can. We had our lives unthreaded by an evil that we could not face until we were forced to. We learned that fear can make you lose your faith in life until you take ownership of fear itself. There are people in all of our lives who help build us up. We should cling to those because for every one of them there is sure to be a demented one trying to crash you down. Hiding from something you are afraid of doesn't make it go away. It just makes it stronger.

Mama and Daddy still live in their house here in Culley Cove. They laugh lots more now than they did for many years. They finally came to terms not only with Jackson's death, but also his murder. We figure it somehow helped to know that Max Gridley lost his manhood off my dock that night at the hands of Gammy.

Mama says she understands my need to find out more about Jackson's end here. I know that if I had told her at the time she would have not had the same attitude. We do what we have to in order to survive.

Wit is still the centerpiece of our lives. He is, if I do say so myself, the most handsome young man that the earth has ever seen. He is now in Culley High and dating the cutest girl. So far, I can't find anything wrong with her, but I am still checkin' into it. He is on medication for his hyperactivity. He has learned to use his like a life skill, as Gammy put it. It makes him the greatest outside-the-box thinker I have ever seen. He enjoys every second of his life. He is loud and spirited and fun, just as Jackson taught me to be. Wit faces reality and enjoys his own conflicts along the way. His view is, you can take me or leave me, but you see what you get. He is so much like Gammy sometimes that I cry laughing.

Uncle Taft finally found his complacency in life. He was true to himself and allowed his family to know his secret. It wasn't easy for all of them, but family is family and acceptance was the end result. Gammy always made it clear that you had to made adjustments in your thinking sometimes when it came to your family. When Taft told her and Pee-Paw gammy gasped and said, "Mercy!" Then she leaned over Uncle Taft asking for some books on the subject. She said that if her son was gay she reckoned she best understand it. Once gammy got the information she needed, she just had a gay son. Her reference to it was no different from one of her sons to have brown hair and the other to have red. No matter what the differences we were all individuals created by God's hand. My uncle frequently visits Culley bringing along his colourful friends. I double dog dare anybody to say a word about it either.

Detective Osbourne moved to Culley Cove and has turned part beach-bum. He and Nita are engaged to be married in a few months. They don't plan to have children. They want to live their lives enjoying each other and the good spirit that Culley exudes.

Gammy and Pee-Paw have never been prouder of a Churchill tale as they were of Gammy's performance that night. Pee-Paw said that he was sure glad he got his money's worth out of the dock he built me.

Uncle Taft tells the story that has become lovingly called the *dock story* perfectly. He says that he had about one minute to call somebody that night while Gridley was telling his sadistic stories. He thought about who he could think of that would move the fastest and get to the dock and help me.

He says Gammy's face appeared in his mind without hesitation. The oldest in the family was the fastest, most high-strung, and the most creative of all.

He says Gammy answered her phone on the first ring that night.

She said, "Hello."

He explained in two sentences that I needed help on the dock.

Gammy said, "I've got it."

Pee-Paw had followed her, asking questions, but she never talked. She went straight to the gun cabinet. She got her rifle while throwing Pee-Paw his. Next, she got out her box of shells. She handed Pee-Paw three shells only. He didn't ask any more questions.

Then she picked up the phone, dialed the police, and quickly said, "Get over to Caroline and Cleeve's dock, now! Call Detective Osbourne in the city and tell him the killer's back," hanging up before a response was given.

She walked, not risking car doors or lights. Pee-Paw crept behind her. She shushed him the entire walk there. Once she reached the dock, she took two steps and crouched down. Then two more steps and crouched down.

She and Pee-Paw knew every creak of that dock. They knew how the wind could move it. Whenever the wind blew just a little, that was their time to step. Max would never know the difference.

When she heard Max making fun of her and taunting me, she lost all sense of reason. Years of rage and denial took over my gammy.

Gammy had always teased us about our secret boxes. She claimed she never understood the big hang-up about them. Right after her heart attack in '04, she asked Pee-Paw to build her one. Neither of them told any of us about it, with the exception of Uncle Skeeter, who had to help her.

A year after Pee-Paw went to the Lord, I was reading to Gammy on her deathbed. She swatted at my hand to stop reading. She looked up and motioned for me to get close to her mouth. Gammy always knew when any of us couldn't face the truth. I had not yet been able to grasp she was about to leave us. Gammy knew I would struggle with her exit from my world.

"Granddaughter, I've been waitin' for several years for this time," she said while coughing into her hand.

"Pee-Paw made me one of them there boxes by the sea whatnots ya'll went so crazy for," Gammy explained.

"Mine is attached to the bottom of your dock, she said. "Skeeter done it for me," she continued. "He is such a handy carpenter like Jesus. He made it so it would attach to the wood on the bottom side of your planks. He tells me it's sealed up tight with plastics. It's safe from rain and the high tide can't reach it. He is to get it down 'cause, Lord knows, only he can. Don't do it until I am gone. Now, make sure I am gone. Have them doctors check my pulse a few times, now," she warned, opening her eyes wide.

"I don't want you to ever hide from your fears again, Caroline. You hear me? Never have fear," she said, giving me a hard look.

"That evil cuss Max Gridley hurt us. He made us scared to live for a while around here. Heck, he even made us scared of each other for a while.

"We started keepin' secrets and hiding our own interests. Taft didn't even tell me, his own mama, about his love of music and that other thang he kept a secret for so long.

On top of that, your poor old mama just about went plumb crazy," she continued.

"Max Gridley almost made you afraid of your own dock, since he haunted you on it. Cleeve tells me you ain't jumped off it since that night. Is that right?" she asked.

"Not yet, but I will," I said.

"*Bull!*" Gammy shot back. She squinted at me.

"Will you ever jump off your dock again and just swim, Caroline?" she asked me.

"Why, Gammy?" I asked.

"'Cause you and I jumped together already when we took that Max on that night," she said with a big Gammy-style laugh.

"We shot his manhood to the sharks," Gammy said, laughing and coughing as I rubbed her back.

"You just remember when you think of him that his balls are in the sea. We puttem there, now didn't we?" she continued.

"Don't you dare let him own even a tiny part of you," she screeched between coughs.

"I know you still see your fancy head doctor, but ya gammy knows about the head too," she said proudly.

"Probably a little more that I want anybody to know I know," she continued with a wink.

"You embrace your dock and the freedom Pee-Paw wanted you to have there. He built it for you to think, relax, and swim from those wooden planks," she explained, looking into my eyes.

"Do you understand, Caroline? Fear nothing," she said, with all of the strength her weakening voice could find.

"Caroline, listen to me. When I'm gone and it won't be long now, get Skeeter, and ya'll go get my box," she said. "Don't stand around this here bed carryin' on like I'm pathetic."

Gammy took in a deep breath so she could talk. "Don't walk around like it's a catastrophe that I'm gone. By the time you start that I will already be working for my boss man, the Lord.

"When Skeeter gets my box down for you, I want you to read it and do what it says right that minute, dear. You hear?" she said, looking at me seriously.

"I'm going to say it again so we make sure there ain't nothin' confusin'. When you open that note from me, you do exactly what it says on there that minute," she repeated.

"I understand, Gammy," I confirmed. "But, Gammy, the doctors aren't telling us that you are..." She cut me off.

"Caroline, I ain't no fool. I don't need no doctor to tell me when it's my time. All I'm doin' right now is tyin' up loose ends and planning on meetin' up with my God, Buckley, and Jackson," she said.

"While you are doin' what my note says, you laugh for me. You make a mind image of all the fun we had here on this Churchill land together. I expect you to keep it going for me, OK?" she said.

"Remember how patient I was with your mama when you are getting to know whoever Wit marries. You have to make exceptions, Caroline. You hold on to your family at all cost. Keep your eye on the ball," she said, grinning at me. "Granddaughter, that is the bottom line when it comes to families.

"Your Wit has the excitement that you, Jackson, and I shared. It's a gift. Never forget that. ADPH or whatever the heck them city folks want to call it. It's the best thing that ever happened to me," she said big eyed.

"ADHD, Gammy," I corrected.

"Oh, who cares what they call it!" she said pointing her finger at me.

"They oughta call it a gift to think outside the box!" That is what it is," she said with her voice fading into a cough.

I could see the fatigue in her face. She reminded me one last time, talking slower now. "Do what I tell you on the note in my box."

Even as bad as she felt, she was grinning just like Jackson had done over giving me the box when I was ten.

Gammy and Jackson were so much alike, and I could feel her walking toward her ending. I knew not to fight it. Death is one true experience that is in God's hands. We can only react to it, never change it.

Gammy Mavis Churchill went to the Lord at 8:39 the next morning. The nurse came in and announced what we knew already by her stillness. I looked at Skeeter over her as she lay silently in that bed.

He looked back at me and simply said, "Come on."

We walked out of the hospital and drove straight to my house. Gammy had been clear about none of us standing over her after she died. She always hated that when she saw it. She never allowed it when Pee-Paw passed either.

The family was waiting there as we were to begin making plans for Gammy's service. Skeeter and I said not one single word in the hospital or in his truck. Gammy was with us somehow, and we both knew it.

Once at my house, we walked out on the long dock until we reached the end. My uncle dropped to his knees then lay on his belly. He was reaching underneath the dock to extract the box. I watched on, still processing that Gammy was really gone. He pulled out the box she had told me about.

It was made so well I knew it could have only been done by Pee-Paw's careful hands. I rubbed my fingers over it, noticing how my hands looked so much like my grandfather's. I held back emotion, because I had learned how over the years. I couldn't allow myself to grieve for Pee-Paw now, as those tears had been shed when he left us.

Mama, Cleeve, Daddy, Wit, Sadie, Taft, and Warren were all in my yard, watching what would later become family tradition. Gammy had reinforced what must happen on the day she left us. She always liked to have her backup plans ready, even in death. They all knew to look on for whatever reason they may have a need.

I swallowed hard, preparing myself to open it. The last words from my gammy were in this box. my anxiousness was rising. Her box, like Jackson's, could speak to me from death and propel me through another stage of my life. I would need her strength and hoped that the words would somehow soothe my heart. I needed her to guide me through this death as she had before.

I had learned from my years with Gammy to always expect the unexpected. She enjoyed that flavor of life. It was the refreshing part of her that kept us all going. Whatever she had for me in her special box could not be predicted. I tried to imagine what she would deem so important for me to know or do. I knew before I opened it that no matter what it said I would do it and do it well. It would be the last thing on this earth I could do for Gammy and that was all I needed to know. She had known this too.

I suppose I was expecting some profound words of wisdom. Maybe even a Bible verse that she had felt I needed to consider throughout the years ahead. Instead, there was one small piece of paper addressed to me. I immediately recognized the handwriting as that of my gammy.

I opened the paper tenderly and began reading it.

Granddaughter,
Jump off your dock now, and I mean it. Swim like a fish back to shore now.
Take this old world by the balls!

All My Love,
Gammy

$\mathcal{A}bout\ the\ \mathcal{A}uthor$

Laurie Hendry Graybar, fifth-generation native of Taylor County, a small rural community outside of Tallahassee, Florida is proud of the south and all of its magnificent culture.

After graduating from Florida State University, she became a teacher in Clay County, Florida and was elected *Teacher of the Year*. She has been instrumental in writing a number of science grants while working with animal rescue projects throughout the state of Florida.

Proving herself as a lifelong learner she spent time in the publishing industry for a Manhattan-based company. Following her creative heart, she became a designer, staging homes, while co-owning an international children's science franchise.

After receiving an adult diagnosis of ADHD (attention deficit hyperactive disorder), she learned first hand about the importance of creative people allowing their curiosity to take on a life of its own. Laurie is a member of the CHADD (children and adults with attention deficit hyperactivity disorder) a non-profit organization. She also holds memberships with a number of writing associations spread across the United States.

She lives in the pines of Tallahassee, Florida with her husband Ben and their two sons. It's her hope that her writing will encourage people to jump from their dock, figuratively and literally.

CPSIA information can be obtained at www.ICGtesting.com
Printed in the USA
LVOW080955230112

265146LV00001B/71/P